THE LAST LUAU

Guy McCullough

Agile Publishing

ISBN: 9798332960215

Printed in the United States of America
Published by Agile Publishing

THE LAST LUAU

by

Guy McCullough

CHAPTER 1

Saturday — December 6, 1941
Honolulu, Territory of Hawaii

T he hand-written letter lay open on my dining room table, amid a stack of bills and sales circulars. On the plain, white sheet of writing paper, each cursive symbol flowed into the next with such uniform perfection it looked as if it had been set in type:

> *Mr. Ross,*
> *I know who killed your partner. My information is worth a lot more than the $1,000 reward you're offering in the newspapers. I read the papers every day. When your offer gets in the ballpark, I shall be in touch.*
> *A Friend*

The envelope was addressed in the same elegant hand to Mac Ross, 3840 Paki Avenue, Honolulu. That meant it couldn't be just another answer to the classified ad I had taken out, offering a reward for information on my partner's murder. My ad listed only my post office box—and no name.

Out the window, the sun was low over Mamala Bay. After a day of rain, the trade winds resumed their duty and blew the last of the Kona weather back over the mountains. Across the street from my house, the royal palms in Kapiolani Park cast long, purple shadows.

Archers gathered their arrows from the range and began packing up their equipment, but on the far side of the park, the cricket club was still hard at it, running around in their whites and shouting to each other. This time of year, they played right up until the very instant the ball disappeared. To the east, the lower slopes of Diamond Head bathed in dark shades of cadmium yellow.

I stood for a moment to watch the sun set on another birthday—my forty-second. The problem was my heart wasn't in it. I was born to a tired woman at the end of a tired century, and it seemed lately that all that exhaustion, held at bay for so long, was starting to catch up with me.

It had been a rough year.

In September, my girlfriend decided she'd had enough of my various prevarications and decamped to California. By Thanksgiving, we stopped writing altogether. In October, my business partner went and got his head blown off with a shotgun. More than a month later, I still had no idea who had done it. For most people, that wouldn't present a problem, but I make my living as a private investigator, and once upon a time I was a police detective, so the whole situation didn't reflect very favorably on me or my abilities.

Still, I had a little money in my pocket, and I decided to go out for dinner, maybe listen to some music, and try to celebrate another trip around the sun. I poured myself a rye and soda, dropped a Cab Calloway record, and smoked the better half of an Old Gold. By the time I'd showered and shaved, I felt like I just might be up to old Cab's challenge to "keep that hi-de-hi deep down in your soul."

A splash of Old Spice, a pair of linen pants, and a clean camp shirt made me begin to feel like a new man. Or at least a newer version of the old one, which would have to do. I laced up my best pair of shoes—two-tone Gatsby brogans, bought with the money from the Hanover case. They felt expensive, but I had to admit they made me look more respectable and I realized that I had coaxed myself into a rosier outlook.

Even so, my mind kept coming back to the anonymous letter. The more I pondered it, the more my gut told me there wasn't a chance in hell the writer had anything of value to sell me. It had to be some sort of shakedown racket. But a little voice in the back of my head had a different opinion. I looked at the stamp. It hadn't been cancelled. The letter had been hand delivered to the box on my front door sometime in the last twenty-four hours. The hit of adrenaline agreed with the voice in my head.

I put the letter and envelope in the safe and told myself there was nothing to be done about it tonight. The next deadline for the *Star-Advertiser* classifieds was Monday afternoon at four.

It was the perfect evening for a ride on my Indian Four motorcycle, a prized possession, and a great way to get around on Oahu. I kicked the starter, and the bike gave its familiar mild roar then settled down to a whisper. From the zoo across the park, I heard a tiger answer back indignantly. I took it as a good omen. Turns out, that was a mistake.

#

The moon, artificial in its perfection, hung above Diamond Head like a Japanese woodcut—hard edges filled with dusty washes of color. Near the golf course, I heard a pueo calling for his mate, discreetly but not without a certain confidence—"Who-who-who-who-WHO?"

It's said the little owl with short ears can rescue souls from the underworld and safely guide armies to victory. I thought about pulling over to see what he could do for an aging man on a motorcycle, but then the lights of downtown Honolulu came more fully into view.

As I turned onto Kalakaua, the crowds of servicemen in their uniforms grew denser, a solid mass of blue, ochre, and white all blending together. The whole island was filling up with *malihini*—newcomers. The place was beginning to feel stuffy and overcrowded in a way that stifled the native culture and serenity.

On the sidewalk in front of Wo Fat, Gus attacked his accordion with the usual verve and fervor, as much a fixture of the place as the green dragon-scale roof tiles or the red dugongs. I dropped a couple of singles into his case, and he acknowledged it, eyes alight, without missing a note of "Jeanette."

I squeezed in the door and through the crowd, equally divided between *haoles*, second generation Japanese Americans (known as *nisei*), and native Hawaiians. Most locals of Chinese descent didn't consider Wo Fat to actually *be* Chinese food. Through the blue cigarette haze, I saw Tommy Ford at the bar, waving his hand to get my attention. Getting there was like swimming against a rip current; I had to move laterally before I could break out and reach the shore. Ford stood up, offering a hand, and gesturing to a freshly poured drink.

"Happy Birthday, Mac. I'm assuming you're not too old now to drink a little whiskey."

"Not 'til they put me in the cold, hard ground, partner, and I'm counting on you to slip in a fresh one right before they nail the lid shut."

I offered him a cigarette, but he shook his head and raised his glass.

"Here's to Mac Ross. The best damn detective and partner a guy could have. Just don't tell Bing Williams I said so."

"That's mighty kind of you," I said, taking a drink. "You know, you're not nearly as big an asshole as I remember you being when we worked together at HPD."

Ford grinned his lopsided grin and said, "Man, we had some times, didn't we?"

"Indeed, we did. Though I notice you didn't say *good* times. But speaking of good times, how are you getting along with Chief Michaels these days?"

He snorted. "That prick? You can't really get along with him. I'm just angling for a posture of benign neglect." He took a long tug at his drink, as an antidote to the mention of the big boss. "He asked about you the other day."

I was surprised and showed it. "About me?"

"He wanted to know if you've dug up a solid lead in the Heston case. I told him if you had any idea who killed Hes

Heston, you would have told me. You wouldn't leave me with my tits hanging out, right? After all, it is my case, technically speaking."

"Of course not. I don't have a thing, Tommy, except I had another anonymous letter in the mailbox today. This one demanded a bigger reward, but then it does have better penmanship."

Ford pointed his trigger finger at me. "I still say the wife did it. That quarter million-dollar life insurance policy she had just taken out, using a power of attorney, was one hell of a coincidence, and you know what I think of coincidences when murder is involved."

"Yeah, there's no such thing," I said. "Except couples in Hawaii use powers of attorney all the time, especially when one of them travels to the mainland on a regular basis like Hes did. And then there's the fact that Marcia Heston was playing bridge the afternoon Hes was shot."

"Yeah, but—"

"With Admiral and Mrs. Kimmel, no less," I said.

"She could have hired it done. A quarter of a million dollars is a lot of motivation. You can *buy* opportunity, Mac. You taught me that."

He had a point.

From the bar, I looked across the immense dining room, wreathed in cigarette smoke so thick it turned the plum-colored columns the shade of a livid bruise. Red dragons on vivid green murals looked down on Wo Fat's dinner crowd with obvious disappointment. The hubbub of conversation reached a new crescendo. I leaned in so I didn't have to shout at Ford.

"I did see Marcia out one night, not long ago, dancing with a bird colonel. They seemed to know each other pretty well. So, I did some checking, but the colonel didn't even have orders for Hawaii until after Hes was shot. And he hadn't been out of Panama for two solid years before that. Unless the colonel is an extraordinarily seductive pen pal, I got nothing, Tommy."

Ford caught the bartender's eye, gestured for another

round.

"Let me get these," I said.

"No way in hell I'm letting the birthday boy buy the drinks. Or the dinner, for that matter."

"The only other thing I've dug up is that Hes wired a quarter of a million dollars to an account at Hibernia Bank, in Frisco. I've got a guy working it from that end, but so far we don't even know who the owner of the account is."

Tommy didn't seem to be paying much attention. "What do you say we eat here at the bar and save some time? I'm playing golf at 0700 in the morning."

#

After the meal and the obligatory fortune cookies (mine assured me "You will discover the truth in time") I tried to convince Ford to go with me to see a band at the Royal Hawaiian Hotel. He insisted nothing must be allowed to get in the way of his Bermuda grass worship service, so after giving him some reasonably good-natured ribbing about liking a silly game more than dancing with women, I hopped on the Indian and headed back in the direction of Waikiki.

It was after ten, but the town was still juking and jiving. For as long as I could remember, it had been fashionable for Honolulu residents to complain about what a sleepy little backwater the town was. Except now it was starting to wake up, and that wasn't going over too well either.

At the Royal, I made my way inside and toward the muffled voice of a crooner singing "If Tomorrow Starts Without Me." I grimaced at his schmaltzy interpretation. If only the song had started without him, too. Just outside the ballroom, there were stacks of dress uniform hats on a long table. Inside, a matching set of older, pasty-faced officers dancing mechanically with their elaborately coiffured wives and a few dozen sunburned tourist couples sagging under the weight of their leis and holiday fun. The flowers fought a losing battle with the smell of bay rum, talcum powder, and old money.

The first people I recognized were Marcia Heston and her bird colonel, coming off the dance floor, Marcia leading the way. I wondered what Ford would think of *that* coincidence. Marcia and I nodded to one another from across the room and when the ruddy faced colonel saw it, he lost a bit of his ruddiness and flashed a nervous smile, apparently unsure of how exactly I might fit into her life. Marcia was tall and blonde. He was short and at least fifteen years older.

The band began to play "Begin the Beguine," a personal favorite, but I didn't see anyone who looked like a good candidate for a dance partner. Until I felt a touch, and there was Marcia.

She tugged my arm, "He's gone to the head. Come dance with me."

"Okay."

She smelled like Shalimar, and she could foxtrot like Eleanor Powell. But the exertion didn't keep her from talking, blonde hair bobbing and swaying.

"A man came by the house yesterday, asking a lot of questions."

I tried to concentrate on keeping the rhythm.

"Really? What about?"

"About Hes. He's a cop from Frisco. Said they had two murders there just like Hes' and would I mind answering some questions. Didn't really seem to go anywhere, though," she said.

"Did you get his name?"

"He left me his card. I'll drop it by your office on Monday."

"And what would you like me to do about it?"

"Just check him out. Make sure he is who he says he is. The more I've thought about it, Mac, the creepier he seemed."

"Sure, I'll check him out. Speaking of Frisco, you remember that private eye friend of mine I hired?"

"Yes."

"He finally found the hotel Hes stayed at when he was there in September—The Coronado on Powell Avenue. Did you guys ever stay there when you were in Frisco together?"

"No. I've never even heard of The Coronado. Hes was more

of a Palace Hotel kind of guy."

"Well, The Coronado is where the trail went cold. And apparently, it's no Palace."

She looked at me. "This must be costing you a small fortune, Mac."

"Well, it won't be costing me anything much longer, if we don't come up with a lead. My guy is showing Hes' photograph to cabbies. But if he doesn't turn up something soon, I guess we'll have to call it quits."

She frowned. "Oh, Mac, don't waste your good money on Hes. He's gone. And you know good and well he wouldn't have spent any on you."

"I can't help it, Marcia. It's what I do."

Mercifully, the dance wound down before I ran completely out of breath. I bowed, as if to imply I could keep dancing like this all night.

"At your service, Mrs. Heston," I said.

She laughed her familiar contralto laugh. "Thanks, Mac. You're a swell guy. Hes was lucky to have you as a partner. I still marvel at the fact someone like you could work with someone like Hes."

While I struggled to come up with something that wouldn't make me sound like a heel, Marcia smiled and walked toward the table where the colonel stood stiffly at attention.

The crooner came back onstage, and I took it as my cue to leave the party that never was. All that Shalimar and feminine energy made me think about paying a visit to The Bronx, my favorite of Honolulu's little houses of joy. It was, after all, my birthday.

#

I cruised up Hotel Street, the center of Honolulu's carefully regulated red-light district, the bike purring softly. The business of love in the Paradise of the Pacific was unlike any other port of call the Navy had ever taken me to. For starters, the entire thing was run almost entirely by women. No pimps. Even the bouncers at many of the houses were women.

From my days with the Honolulu Police Department, I knew that the predominant view held by the ruling *haoles* went something like this: prostitution has always existed, and it always will. In a city where the men so thoroughly outnumber the women, it's impossible to put a stop to it. Better to have regulated houses with strict rules than have our pure wives and daughters defiled by hordes of randy young soldiers, sailors, and Marines.

No one claimed it was morally defensible. But most admitted it was eminently practical. Especially the commanders of the garrison and the fleet, who could boast the lowest venereal disease rates in the US armed forces. The money to be made, well, that made everyone happy once it had time to work its way around town. Those at the top of the money pyramid were especially content: the madams (who made out like bandits), the women (who could earn ten times the wages of a secretary), and the beat and vice cops, who got slipped a picture of President Jackson every now and then to look the other way on little things, like closing time or the occasional whiff of *pakalolo* smoke.

The Bronx, where I had paid a few visits since my girlfriend left me in the fall, was run with the efficiency of an infantry brigade by a madam who had honed her craft in old New Orleans, a major league town where brothels are concerned. But she was not the madam from central casting. As wiry as a rail-splitter, Mary Nell didn't tipple all night, though she did chain-smoke Chesterfields, lighting one from the smoldering remnants of the last. She lived upstairs with her lesbian lover, Kai, a big-boned Hawaiian *wahine* who worked as the joint's bouncer.

Like all good managers, Mary Nell was firm but fair to everyone involved: the girls, the staff, the customers. "Can't you see I'm trying to run a reputable house of ill repute here?" was her frequent admonition to minor transgressors.

She gave me a rare smile when I came through the door.

"Well, look what the cat dragged in. We were hoping you would grace us with your presence on the day of your nativity, Mac."

"How did you know it was my birthday?"

She laughed. "I don't know everything, but I make it my business to know *almost* everything. Nalani told me. It's her day off, but she said to call her when you came in."

"*When* I came in? I really hadn't planned on it," I said.

Mary Nell snorted. "Nalani's mother is a seer. Nalani gets it from her; she knows things. I suggest you keep that in mind," she said, the smile returning. "But tonight, you must banish care." She cocked her head toward the stairs. "Go on up to Nalani's room. Last on the right. We can't have you using a cubicle on your birthday. A man of your age needs room to do his business. I'll send up a bottle of champagne."

"What's got into you?"

"I've always been a loving creature," she said.

"I may have to consider having birthdays more often, if this is the treatment I get."

"Consider? Ha! They'll come plenty often from here on out," she called up the stairs.

Under House Rule Number One, the upstairs was strictly off limits to the customers. The ragtime rhythm of the piano faded behind me. It was much quieter, more of a female enclave up here, like a boarding house that catered strictly to the fairer sex.

I found Nalani's room, neatly appointed in an eclectic style. I put the money on the dresser and stretched out along the bed, propped up by the headboard, trying to look nonchalant. In due course, the champagne arrived, delivered by a steward who put his finger over his lips conspiratorially. I had just picked up a LIFE magazine when I heard footsteps in the hall.

Nalani Castelo appeared in the doorway, gracefully at ease, her tall figure draped in a batik sarong. Around each wrist was a green bracelet of woven ferns. Her dark, slightly wavy hair fell in front of her shoulders to the height of her breasts. Behind her right ear, a single red plumeria with a brilliant yellow center. In that moment, she was the goddess Hina, the first *wahine*, at the very instant of creation.

She lingered for an instant, left arm braced high against the doorframe to feature the fern bracelet, allowing me to take in her divine presence. The effect was stunning, and she knew it. All I could think of was that, at last, I fully understood what old Bill Shakespeare meant when he wrote, "It is the east and Juliet is the sun." I felt as if I could arise and kill the moon, the stars, and half the guys in Honolulu, if that's what it took.

Breaking the pose, Nalani kicked off her shoes and glided on bare feet to the dresser. Her complexion was flawless, skin the color of honey, when the bees have been into the orange blossoms.

She spoke with delight in her voice. "I got you a present, Mac." She picked up a ten-inch record and held it carefully by the edges of the cover for my inspection. "It's Julio Cueva," she said.

"How did you—where did you find it?"

She was pleased that I was pleased. "At the Shellac Shack, you know the one. On King Street? My cousin Tony works there. He helped me pick it out. I told him you like Latin and Caribbean music."

"You amaze me. Thank you. It's the best present. Ever."

She opened the phonograph and placed the record on the spindle. "El Marañon," an old standard, began to play. She danced slowly, sinuously across the floor toward me. When she reached the bed, she worked some sort of magic that made the sarong fall away with the flick of a wrist. She knelt on the bed beside me and, when I opened my mouth to speak, put two fingers to my lips in a shushing motion.

In the light, her intelligent brown eyes shone brightly, irregular flecks of green around the irises. She smelled of sandalwood, vanilla, and heaven. She began to unbutton my shirt.

The next thing I knew, Señor Cueva was grooving on "Tingo Talango," and Nalani and I found a syncopated rhythm that was all our own.

Skin along skin. Bone atop bone. Sinew around sinew. A distant part of me wondered whether time was standing still, or if it had been stretched so long and so far, I couldn't feel it move anymore. The waves rose and crested, rose and crested, before slowly, ineluctably breaking on the shore.

When we were both spent, we lay entwined, the only sound the susurrus of our breathing and the rhythmic scratch of the record needle, darting back and forth in the final groove. I looked at Nalani. She looked at me.

"Happy Birthday, Mac," she said in a husky whisper.

#

It wasn't until I was outside and back on the bike that I realized, while searching for my lighter, that Nalani, through some sleight of hand, had put the money I had left for her back in my pocket. For the time it took the thought to cross my mind, I considered going back in to leave it with Mary Nell but realized that would just cause problems for everyone. Not to mention, it would be an insult to a woman who had given me something no amount of money could touch.

I cranked the Indian and idled out to Hotel Street. It was just turning midnight and the streets were still full of sailors and soldiers, a lucky few with dates. There were two ways I could go at this juncture in history: right or left.

Right would take me the thirty miles to my little beach shack at Haleiwa on the North Shore, where I planned to spend the night, so that I could go surf fishing early the next morning before the winter waves grew too intense. Left would take me past (and presumably to) most of my favorite watering holes. I idled for a moment at the intersection, the bike patiently humming beneath me. Ah, hell. It was my birthday. How many more could I count on?

I turned left.

The first stop was a little place called The Blue Lagoon. Then the The Top Hat. At Glenn O'Hara's, they were stacking chairs, but let me have one for the road, since I was a regular.

Around 1:30, a bit wobbly, I pointed my iron steed toward the North Shore. Thankfully, the Indian knew the way home of its own accord. It carried me quickly up the valley, past Wheeler Airfield. Through the fence, I could see the P-40s huddled wingtip to wingtip, a defense against sabotage.

I floated along in a state of bliss, my heart rising with every warp and woof, leaning into the turns, feeling the alternating pockets of warm and cool air, each with its own distinct floral bouquet.

There are times of great peril in life, as it turns out, when you start to believe that the universe is organized purely for your joy and pleasure. The fog lifts, the moon shines through, the night rainbow appears in the sky, and the woman comes to your bed. That's when it becomes all too easy to begin thinking that life, like Hawaii, is a paradise. That's when you're in trouble.

On the beach in Haleiwa, my Puerto Rican neighbors were hosting a wedding luau, a stone's throw from my little house. The sound of the music and laughter would have been irresistible, never mind the social obligation, even at 2 o'clock in the morning.

The party guests were a living representation of the successive waves of immigrants lured to the islands to work the sugar cane and the pineapple: Chinese, Japanese, Filipino, Korean, and Portuguese. Even Norway was represented, by the Karlsen Brothers, Lars and Stig, on trumpet and trombone. They were playing *kachi-kachi* music as tightly as if they had been born in old San Juan.

I was barely off the bike before someone handed me a can of Schlitz, as cold as the Pacific could make it. A heaping plate of food appeared, unbidden. Roasted Kalua pig (the most essential luau food), squid, poi from the taro root, laulau, and lomilomi salmon. But there was also a Filipino ox-tail stew, bratwurst, burgers, and hot dogs.

We all danced and sang and offered endless toasts to the wedding couple until the band broke into "Lagrimas Negras," a heart-breaking song about love and betrayal and abandonment. No one seemed to notice or care it was about black tears.

When I could politely slip away, I pushed the bike across the road to the house, not trusting myself to mount, let alone ride it. I parked it around back, by the kitchen door, so no one would come calling too early in the morning. Something told me surf fishing at dawn was no longer on the schedule.

Stumbling into the galley kitchen, I found the water jug and drank as much as I could, offering a wordless apology to my liver. The only sound was the aqueous bubbling of my Adam's apple and my deep breaths between gulps. I tumbled into bed, barefoot but otherwise fully clothed. I fell asleep with "Lagrimas Negras" playing in my slightly spinning head.

Toward morning I dreamt I was walking near an unfamiliar shore. Suddenly, I plunged into a dark pit, from which I knew, as one knows things in a dream, that I could never hope to escape. Lucidly, I expected to awaken when I hit bottom but, for once, it failed to happen. Then, the pit and the sky and the world were swallowed by an immense pall of black smoke.

#

I woke up around six, parched and frowzy. In the kitchen I poured a glass of water and drank it down, catching a glimpse of the bike out the window in its unfamiliar place. The expensive brogans were wrapped around the handlebars, shoelaces intertwined, a sandy sock stuffed into each shoe. I lurched out the door to retrieve them in the gathering light.

The sky on Oahu is a living, breathing quotidian being, as real as your neighbor, or your lover, or yourself. Few places can rival it. Certain parts of the American west. The Alps. The Atacama Desert in Chile and Peru.

I paused for a moment to take it in, along with a deep breath of hibiscus-scented air. I went back inside, drank all the water I could manage, took off my clothes, and crawled back into bed. Sleep came instantly and I descended into the depths.

#

CHAPTER 2

Beethoven, Herr Schindler tells us, intended the opening of his Fifth Symphony to be the sound of Fate knocking on the door. While I was sleeping it off, Fate came knocking for everyone. In my case, it even waited patiently for me to wake up and answer.

I ignored the first few knocks, but when they became insistent, I tumbled out of bed.

"Coming!"

I threw on a robe, fished a cigarette from the pack in the pocket, lit it with a shaky hand, and opened the door. At the bottom of my short stoop stood my friend and neighbor, Akira Tinaka, a favorite teacher to many a North Shore kid. He bowed.

"Mr. Ross-san," he said, unusually formal.

"Please, Akira, call me Mac."

"I would not show my face this morning if I did not require your assistance, Ross-san. My cousin Daniel has been murdered."

"What?"

"He was walking to his girlfriend's house in Pacific Heights, around midnight last night. Shot in the head, sir. You must help me. My family—we don't know what to do."

I invited him in. He stood awkwardly just inside the door.

"Can I offer you something to drink?

He appeared not to hear me.

"Daniel Nakajima is his name. He is—he was—my uncle's son, my cousin. A teacher like me. I am ashamed to ask on this of all days, but we don't know where to begin, Mac."

Akira was a handsome man, his intelligent eyes framed by

round tortoise-shell glasses, hair the color of coal, slicked back neatly. By all accounts he was a captivating teacher, but standing forlornly in my living room, he looked like a lost child.

"First of all, there's nothing to be ashamed of, Akira. I try not to work on Sunday, but half the time I end up doing something anyway. It's no big deal," I said.

The color drained from Akira's face.

"Oh, Ross-san, I'm not ashamed of that. I—my family and I—and everyone I know are ashamed of what Japan has done today." He glanced at the silent radio. "Have you not heard?"

Akira sat down heavily. "They have attacked us all over the island, Mac. Pearl, Kaneohe, Hickham, Schofield. Even Wheeler."

It was my turn to sit. I thought immediately of Nalani.

"Ross-san. May I have a glass of water, please? I don't feel well."

I poured him a tall glass from the tap, adding a little whiskey, flinching slightly at the smell of it. Akira stared into the middle distance as he steadily drank it down.

#

The rye revived Akira enough for me to get him moving, and I may even have begun to convince him that he and his family bore no responsibility for Emperor Hirohito's foreign policy. I promised to try to get Daniel's body released for a timely funeral, always a matter of importance in Japanese culture. I told Akria to ask Hosoi Chapel, the family's funeral home of choice, to show up at the morgue and ask for the remains. If Akira was right about the scale of this air raid, there could be scores of *nisei* dead. They were, after all, the most populous ethnic group on Oahu. He walked backward out the door, bowing and thanking me, and breaking my heart.

I turned on the radio and turned the dial to KGMB. They were playing music. Maybe Akira had it all wrong, but I somehow doubted it. I dressed quickly in a light, long-sleeved shirt, chinos and sturdy boots.

As the song finished, the familiar voice of Web Edwards

came from the Philco.

"Repeating what we know at this hour. Oahu has been attacked by the Japanese from the air. This is not a drill. It's the real McCoy. All service personnel are to report to their units at once. Civilian residents should remain where you are unless you have essential duties to perform. Stay off the roads. Stay home and out of the Army and Navy's way. An invasion by forces of the Empire of Japan remains a very real possibility. Blood donations are needed at all area hospitals. A blackout and curfew will begin at 6:30pm this evening and remain in force until dawn. No light whatsoever may be shone."

Then, inexplicably, more music—the kind of slack key guitar tune you would expect to hear on any Sunday morning. I found the big thermos and filled it with water. Retrieved a carton of Old Golds from the kitchen cabinet. I wolfed down two hard boiled eggs and a piece of leftover Opakapaka.

The music ended abruptly. "Ladies and gentlemen, I've just received word that KGMB and all stations in the Territory of Hawaii will cease broadcasting at this time."

After a few seconds of dead air, the carrier dropped. Static and atmospheric pops and whistles took over, as if civilization itself had winked out, like a guttered candle. I turned off the radio and gathered my bundle. *I hope there's enough gas in the bike.*

Stay off the roads and give blood, the man said. Well, it was impossible to do both. The tank was more than half full. I cranked the machine. Its reassuring roar was heartening.

Pulling away, I saw Peter Ochoa and a group of neighbors on the beach, rifles in hand, looking seaward. I stopped within shouting distance and cupped my hand.

"I'm going to Schofield to give blood. Maybe downtown if I can get there. I'll be back before dark to take my turn on the beach. The Springfield is in the shack if you need it before then."

Ochoa waved the rifle above his head and shouted back.

"Thanks, Mac. We'll be right here. If they have the *cohones* to come back, we'll bury the bastards."

#

It wasn't a long ride to Schofield, but it was long enough to see that Akira was right. The planes I had seen parked cheek by jowl at Wheeler the night before were now a twisted mass of metal and ash. I tasted the burnt tang of it all the way across the field. The "defense" against sabotage had ensured not one plane got off the ground.

Schofield, the largest base anywhere under the U.S. flag, was normally a picture of perfection, each rock painted the same shade of white and placed perfectly in alignment with its neighbors. Yesterday at this time, every lawn and shrub and building would have been all spit and polish, ready to pass inspection by the most fastidious general. Now it was a wreck.

At the base hospital, the lightly injured were mixed together on the front lawn with the dead and dying. The line to give blood stretched around the building, almost doubling back on itself. I saw Vassar and Betty from The Bronx on the lawn, comforting the wounded. Vassar, who must have had some medical training somewhere in her rollicking adventure of a life, was expertly dressing a corporal's arm. Everybody called her Vassar because she graduated, *summa cum laude* no less, from that tony college, and she had the sheep skin to prove it. Right away, I could see the ladies of The Bronx had an ease and an instant rapport with the men that even some nurses seemed to lack.

A nurse approached, gave the corporal an injection, and marked his forehead with a bright red "M" in lipstick, then moved on to the next man moaning in pain. I closed my eyes for a moment and listened to the soul-killing cries. From what I could see, they were going to run out of morphine long before they ran out of lipstick.

It was maddening to just stand still and wait. But it was the one thing I could do that would help, so as soon as they let me go, I refilled my thermos from the water fountain and got back in line. Once upon a time, the Navy had given me enough medical training to know that I could spare at least one more pint.

Waiting gave me time to think about the most recent anonymous letter. I kept coming back to the use of "newspaper," and "I shall." That could mean it was written by someone who was well-educated. The same was true of "in the ballpark," on the one hand an idiomatic phrase that was thoroughly American. On the other, the kind of thing a non-native English speaker eager to assimilate might incorporate into their speech. One thing was certain; the uniform lettering was an ingenious way to obscure the source—better even than words cut out of magazines. The perfectly formed copybook letters were inscrutable.

Everybody in town seemed to be in the line to give blood. A short Chinese woman with a parasol stood next to a towering Hawaiian in a mechanic's uniform. There were air crews who no longer had a plane to tend to. Office workers. And a group of men in unfamiliar uniforms who turned out to be a Dutch ship captain and his crew. By the time I got back to the head of the line, the nurses were marking every donor's right thumb with indelible blue ink.

Vassar walked across the lawn and held up her thumb.

"I regret that I have but one pint to give for my country," she said with a tired smile.

"For somebody, it will make all the difference. Have you seen Nalani today?"

"No, she went to her mom's house after you left last night. Say, Mac, this probably doesn't matter now, but there was a guy asking about you at the Bronx not long after. They call him 'Money,' but he didn't look like money to me."

"I don't believe I've had the pleasure of meeting Mr. Money. What did he look like?"

"Loud. Really loud. Loud clothes. Loud mouth. About my height. A bit of a greaser with the hair he has left. He's what we gals call 'dye it black and comb it back.'"

"He sounds delightful. But not really my type."

"He's not anybody's type. You know Mary Nell lets us refuse clients at the Bronx, right? Well, Money literally can't get laid in a cat house."

I shook my head in sadness. "Thanks for the heads up. I'll check him out."

"You bet."

I couldn't do anything but get in the way at Schofield, so I headed downtown in the hope of finding something useful to do. Along the way, I saw a downed Japanese zero and passed through two checkpoints, both manned by ROTC members from the University of Hawaii, almost all of whom were *nisei*. At each point they looked me over carefully to make sure I was who my driver license said I was: Macdonald J. Ross, brown hair, blue eyes, six feet two inches, weight one hundred ninety pounds. It was all true, except maybe for the last part.

When I finally made it to The Bronx, I found it unlike I had ever seen it—empty and as quiet as a tomb. In Nalani's room, dust motes floated slowly in the still air above a single chrysanthemum in a tiny vase. On the mirror, in lipstick: "Gone to Hospital Point to help out."

Back on the bike, I stopped to pick up an ensign from the *USS Shaw*. Maybe I wasn't the only one who had slept through it all.

"Take me to Pearl, mister," he said. "I've got to get back to my ship and check on my buddies."

Near the main gate at Pearl, traffic began to back up. So much for everyone staying off the roads. People were coming to help and to hell with the roads. We pulled opposite Battleship Row, and the boy jumped off.

Here was the dreaded abattoir. Twisted, broken metal and twisted, broken men. It had been hours since the attack ended, but bodies still floated in the water between the shore and Ford Island. The branches of a banyan tree were stuffed, here and there, with large body parts, like a surrealist landscape painting.

I'd seen dead and dying men in the last war, when my destroyer took a torpedo from a German U-Boat. As we sank, our depth charges started going off. In eight minutes, the old swayback went down, leaving more than sixty men dead.

The sight and smell of the bodies being pulled into the duty boats brought back the horror. In each boat, they were stacked like mannequins, if the mannequins are missing a lot of their parts. I felt the bile rise in the back of my throat.

I saw four Japanese airmen in their blue uniforms, their bodies laid out apart from the Americans. One still wore his helmet. Along the waterfront, exhausted GIs covered in oil, many burned or injured, huddled in dispirited groups. The light had gone out of their eyes. The next three hours were a blur of dazed sailors and airmen as I helped them to a make-shift hospital somebody had set up in an empty hangar. The entire time I was hoping I might see Nalani.

Every few minutes, some poor bastard would pull me aside to let me in on the latest crazy scuttlebutt: Japanese parachutists were landing at Kapolei; their carriers had been sighted off Barber's Point; a Japanese marine division was coming ashore at Kahuku, an extraordinarily bad place to land one.

Toward the end of the day, as the sun sank toward the water, I helped a black Army sergeant change a tire on his two-and-a-half-ton truck. His uniform hung from him in shreds. He had a broken arm held up in a sling, a nasty cut all along his collarbone, and a look of grim determination on his face.

When the sergeant had gone, struggling to steer the big truck with his good arm, I sat with my back to a scorched palm and had a good cry, watching black smoke from the *Shaw* boiling into the sky. I craved a cigarette, but I'd given away the whole carton.

After my water ran out, I had a lukewarm Coca-Cola, taken from a case of them left sitting in the sun by hands unknown. The thought of food never occurred to me. I just kept looking for useful things to do and then doing them. Native Hawaiians speak of a magic leaf that relieves all hunger and thirst, but I think in my case it was pure adrenaline and a searing hatred of the Empire of Japan.

I had to get back before the blackout, so I went looking for Nalani. At Hospital Point, I found a roach coach serving sandwiches, free for the asking. Something told me we wouldn't be calling them that anymore for a long time to come. I took one for Nalani.

I found her in the auditorium, cradling the head of an injured G.I. and giving him water from a tin cup. He was so blackened from head to toe, his watery eyes stood out like searchlights. When the tears rolled down his face, they turned black from the oily soot.

Nalani's white shirtwaist dress was covered in broad streaks of rusty blood. Her right thumb was blue. When she saw me, she smiled wanly. When the water ran out, she came to me.

Her eyes filled with tears. "What are we to do now, Mac?" she asked.

I wiped a smudge of oil from her brow. "I wish I knew."

#

I thought I had left myself enough time before the blackout to send a telegram to the county coroner about the disposition of Daniel Nakajima's body, but one look at the line at the Western Union office on King Street and I knew that wouldn't work.

The Honolulu Police Department had its own telegraph office that fed directly into the system, so I pulled in there instead, slipping in the open back door. Tommy Ford wasn't in his office, or the detective's room. I found him manning the phones out front still dressed in plus-fours ready for the links. He waved and pulled a face, gesturing to the phone.

"Ma'am, I'm sorry, but we can't deal with that at the moment. I'm going to have to ask you to call back in a few days, please." He paused to listen. "Ma'am, there's a war on, haven't you heard?"

He put the phone back in the cradle with some force behind it. "Judas Priest. Crazy broad says someone stole five dollars from her handbag while she was in the ladies' loo last night at Chez Paree. She's pretty sure it was the hat check girl. Can you believe it? Damn, Mac, you look like hell warmed over."

"I've been there and back again. I suggest you avoid the harbor if you can. Take the worst crime scene you've ever seen and multiply by a few thousand. Listen, I need to send a cable, do you mind?"

Ford said, "Of course not. You still remember how to do it, right?"

"Thanks, I can manage."

"What's it about? Not that it matters. But it may take a while to go out."

"I'm trying to help the Nakajima family. Their son, Daniel, was murdered last night up in Pacific Heights."

Ford's eyes widened. "I haven't seen anything on that."

The phone rang. He held up a finger, lifted the receiver. "Honolulu Police Department, Detective Ford speaking."

I sent the cable and dropped back by the duty desk on the way out.

"Thanks, buddy. I owe you one."

"You owe me a lot more than one, bucko," Ford said. "So, you've been hired to find out who killed the Nakajima lad?"

"The family has asked me to take the case."

Ford shook his head. "Mac, I don't have to tell you no one is going to get too wound up about a dead Japanese boy. Not with hundreds of Americans killed in a Jap sneak attack. Speaking unofficially, of course."

"I don't see why not. It's not Daniel Nakajima's fault. And I'm sure there are plenty of dead *nisei*, too."

"Even so, you know it will be rough sledding, Mac. They've declared martial law, and we've already started rounding up a whole slew of Japanese nationals with strong ties to the homeland. Word is they'll be interned on Sand Island for the duration. Nobody would blame you if you took a pass on this one."

"I know, Tommy."

His phone rang. He let it ring. "Let me know if I can do

anything else to help, partner."

#

I don't remember a great deal about the ride back to the North Shore, except for thinking my presence there wasn't going to be much of a deterrent to any Japanese landing, in the unlikely event one came in such bright moon conditions. My next thought, and they were coming slowly now, was that a Japanese dawn landing the day following the raid, on the other hand, would certainly not be the worst idea since Themistocles withdrew to Salamis.

At the shack on the North Shore, I found a telegram pinned to the door. It was from Kintaro Sato's chief of staff, proposing I meet with Sato-san at ten o'clock the following morning.

Sato was a successful businessman and a patriarch of the Japanese community, who some claimed to be the head of a criminal syndicate. In my ten years at HPD, I had heard a lot of rumors about Sato, but no one had ever been able to pin anything on him. That and the fact that he knew enough about me to send a cable to my surf shack made me a bit uneasy.

I dialed the number on Sato's telegram. A soft-spoken woman answered in perfect English. I told her I would be glad to call on Sato-san at ten, but she insisted a car would pick me up in front of my office.

I retrieved the blackout curtains from the hall closet and filled them to the rods that had been in place for two years now, since the first island-wide drill. When the whole thing was rigged in five minutes flat, it gave me a certain smug satisfaction.

A quick review of the kitchen made it clear my only dinner option was "eggs in a hat," made with the last of the eggs and a couple of pieces of bread that, like me, were barely hanging on. I ate like a wolf, or maybe like a man who had run out of magic leaf. It looked like magic was going to be in short supply for a while.

#

A few minutes before six, I reported to Peter Ochoa on the beach for guard duty. Peter had put up a tent at roughly the midpoint of our one-mile area of responsibility. I came bearing cigarettes, from my last carton, which made me instantly popular. Peter insisted on giving me one of his thin, brown cigarillos in return. They reminded me of my dead partner Hes; he had smoked them like a fiend for years.

Ochoa said, "Once it gets dark, be sure to close the tent flap before you light up."

Peter explained his proposal to our little group, almost all of whom I had seen at the luau. We drew straws and I felt lucky to get the second watch. There was no way I was going to sleep any time soon in my adrenalized state, but if I could make it through the night watch, ending at midnight, I could collapse in a heap and sleep the sleep of the righteous.

Ochoa laid out the rules of engagement and gave a remarkably succinct summary of what he'd been told by the Army from a page of notes. The Japanese task force was believed to be retiring toward Jaluit, in the Marshall Islands; or perhaps toward a point between Wake and Midway; that is, if they were not steaming to launch another attack, somewhere farther south. On the other hand, they could be preparing an amphib operation against Oahu.

"Glad we cleared that up," Ochoa said, with a patient smile.

It was a night of itchy trigger fingers and moon shadows. Every so often, a gunshot or two on one of our flanks. Once it sounded as if it came from somewhere inland and went on for several minutes. When my watch ended, I shook hands and wished everyone good luck and walked back through the darkness to my little hut, where I found another telegram pinned to the door.

Once inside, I pulled the curtains and turned on the

light and the radio. The telegram was from the coroner of Honolulu County: "Received your cable. Body released to Hosoi. COD for Mr. Nakajima was single small-caliber gunshot wound to posterior base of skull. Full report in my office this week. All criminal cases to be given priority. –HALE"

#

As soon as the sun was up, I closed up the beach shack as fast as I could. The hardest part was finding the damned door key. Nobody on the North Shore that I knew locked their door at night.

Across from the house on Paki Avenue, the archery range was already gone from the park. The whole area looked like an armed camp. Another early casualty of war. I hurriedly showered and put on a clean shirt and my best suit and rode downtown.

All along the way, I saw the Japanese stores had taken down their Kanji signs. In front of my building, a newsy who could not have been much older than ten hawked his product at the top of his soprano voice: "Saboteurs land here. Raiders Return in Dawn Attack. Paper, Mister? Just five cents." I didn't believe either story, but I bought one any way.

The door to my office still read "Heston and Ross, Confidential Investigations." Hes had insisted it had to be in that order because it "just didn't sound right the other way around." I made a mental note to get it scraped and repainted.

I read the newspaper through. It was hard to separate fact from speculation and rumor. For starters, it grossly understated the civilian death toll, pegging it at a ridiculously low thirty-seven. I had seen three times the number of dead civilians myself. Today's "dawn attack" couldn't possibly be accurate, either, though I didn't doubt the part about renewed anti-aircraft fire. The Nakajima murder was reported with the police blotter, on page seven.

The names of those killed in the Japanese attack were printed, where names were available. In many cases, there were only descriptions: "unknown male, had initials HAD on shirt pocket, taken to morgue," or "Portuguese girl, age 10, wound left temple." Across the islands today, people were waking to find they had lost a loved one after all.

A few minutes before my appointment with Sato, I went downstairs. I was waiting on the sidewalk when, to the minute, a long black Buick pulled to the curb. It wasn't the flashiest car on Oahu by a long shot, but it was a powerful machine. It looked like a '42 that had just been driven off the showroom floor.

A dapper gentleman in a black suit who looked like a young Toshiro Mifune stepped from the backseat, bowed, and greeted me with a business-like smile.

"Mr. Ross? How do you do? My name is George Koga. I am Sato-san's assistant." He gestured toward the car, "Won't you join me, please?"

The car was so clean and polished, I slid halfway across the backseat. We rode in silence, but not very far—just down a couple of blocks and over three. The entire way, I felt as if the driver was examining me in the rear-view mirror, trying to decide if I was a secret assassin. But it could have been the expensive sunglasses.

The distance between my office building and Sato's, next door to Bishop Bank, was more than one of mere geography. My building was known locally as "the den of thieves," not for anything I had done, but because a number of shyster lawyers favored its affordable rents.

Sato's building had a proper lobby, with large plants in giant urns, expensive furnishings, and high-brow art. We crossed it to a private lift, where Koga used a key to call the elevator car. An operator, wearing a smart, black uniform and dove gray gloves bowed to us and manipulated the door and gears without a word. We ascended smoothly to the penthouse level amid the smell of machine oil and beeswax.

When the operator pulled open the gate, with a flourish like a magician performing a favorite trick, I hesitated for an instant. I had expected to see Asian furnishings, but we might as well have been next door at the bank. Everything looked elegant and expensive, and thoroughly occidental.

In the elevator lobby, three young men in well-tailored suits played mahjong. They stood as we came in. To the trained eye, their jackets concealed shoulder holsters. Koga nodded to them, and they went back to their game.

We passed into an outer office, where a middle-aged woman, also wearing black, rose from a desk to bow and greet us.

"Good morning, Ross-sama. May I get you anything? Coffee, tea?"

Mr. Koga escorted me into the inner office, a vast expanse occupying an entire corner of the place. A distinguished gentleman in a gray suit, wearing a black arm band, rose from behind an immense desk and walked briskly toward us. He looked to be about sixty, with short-cropped, salt-and-pepper hair. He bowed subtly, bending slightly from the waist.

"Ross-sama. Thank you for coming. I am Kintaro Sato, but please call me Kintaro."

We had barely dispensed with the pleasantries before the coffee arrived, steaming hot. Koga's assistant bowed and backed out. I thanked her and watched her go, taking in the office. It was like the lobby, tastefully decorated in a way that could only be called American, right down to the prints on the wall: gentlemen in red coats riding to hounds, wintry scenes engraved by Currier and Ives. On his desk, an elegant silver ink stand looked as if it had cost something approximating my annual income.

On the wall to Sato's left, I saw the unmistakable outlines of where a samurai sword had once hung. Sato caught me looking. Clearly very little escaped him.

"We have painters coming this afternoon. It would seem now is not the time for displaying Japanese cultural artifacts. In fact, before we get down to the business at hand, Mr. Ross, please allow me to convey my deepest sorrow, condolence, and regret for the acts of the Empire of Japan. I am personally no longer allegiant to the emperor. And my organization wishes to dissociate ourselves, most strenuously, from this act of barbarity. He gestured toward a console radio. "President Roosevelt has just called yesterday 'a date which will live in infamy,' and I could not agree more."

"Thank you, sir. I know my *nisei* friends well enough to know they feel the same way."

"I am grateful to you for saying so. It means a great deal to me."

Though seated, I made as if to bow.

Turning to a fresh chapter, Sato said, "Now to business, shall we? I am sure you must be wondering why I asked you here today."

I had an idea, but I said, "Yes, sir."

"I'm told that you have been made aware of the murder, late on Saturday evening or perhaps in the early hours Sunday, of Mr. Daniel Nakajima."

"Yes, sir. His cousin, who is a friend and neighbor, told me. I was very sorry to hear it."

"I thank you for that and for your kindness in helping to get the body released so quickly. I would like to engage your services in investigating—in solving—the murder. The Nakajimas are distant relations, our families came from the same prefecture. Moreover, I have certain," he paused for the first time, searching for the right word, "certain responsibilities to the Japanese community in Hawaii. It is a matter of honor that I do everything within my power to resolve this issue. And I believe, sir, that hiring you is the most likely way to accomplish that objective."

"Well, Mr. Sato, as I told Akira, it will not be an easy thing to do."

"You are correct, sir. It would have been difficult in normal times, and these are no longer normal times. But then again, the Hanover case was not an easy thing, either was it?"

I nodded awkwardly.

"You need not be modest with me, sir. We know about you and your abilities. I should like to hire you to apply those abilities on behalf of the Nakajima family."

"Well, Mr. Sato, a thing like this would, normally, take weeks or maybe months. For starters, there are no witnesses. At least none we know of. But, as you correctly point out, these are not normal times. I wouldn't want to take your money when, chances are, it won't pan out."

Sato sat forward in his chair. "How much money are we talking about, sir?"

Here was my chance to get off the hook. "Well, I normally get $50 a day, plus expenses, and those can add up fast. It's impossible to say, really."

The moment the words were out of my mouth, it occurred to me that a man like Kintaro Sato likely knew exactly how much I normally got. If so, he was far too polite to contradict me.

"And," I said, thinking surely this would cinch it, "It's entirely possible that I might need to bring in associates, depending on how things develop."

Sato sat back again. "How about this, Mr. Ross. Before the close of business today, the Nakajima family will have delivered to your office a check for $1,000 as an advance against your fees and expenses. That should get us started. And if their balance should run low, you need only get in touch with Mr. Koga, and we will replenish the funds. I think it best that I do not pay you directly, not that I am trying to conceal our support, but simply because I don't want you to have to answer awkward questions, from certain quarters, about who your client is."

"Do you think anyone might question where the Nakajimas got so much money?"

He made a dismissive motion with his finely manicured hand. "Let them wonder. But you might be surprised by the resources even modest Japanese families have husbanded, Mr. Ross. We are a frugal people, to the degree one can make such generalized statements."

"Well, I didn't mean—"

"No, of course not, sir. No indeed. Just to ensure you that we are fully committed to this undertaking, I am also prepared to pay you a bonus of $2,500 for information leading to the arrest and conviction, and so on and so forth. And I can also have my associates make all the arrangements for you to interview Daniel's family and friends, his girlfriend, and anyone else you might find helpful within the Japanese community."

"That's very generous, sir." Having insulted the entire Japanese diaspora, by implying they all lived in penury, I didn't think it right to add that there was only the slimmest chance I would ever collect the bonus. "May I take some time to think about it?"

Sato said, "Of course," as if only a fool would agree on the spot. "Just let me know by two o'clock this afternoon if you don't mind. So that I can make the financial arrangements before the banks close. There's talk they may not open again for days."

I looked at the clock on the wall. It was pushing eleven.

"There is one more factor you should consider, Mr. Ross."

"Yes, sir?"

"If you find Daniel Nakajima's murderer, I will tell you who killed your partner."

I felt a tightening in the pit of my stomach. I'd put aside a hard-earned grand in hopes of finding my partner's murderer. Here was the chance to solve it, save the thousand, and to get paid rather handsomely in the meantime. There were a million questions I wanted to ask, but this was not the time to ask them. There was a simple offer on the table, and it didn't include Sato answering questions. Sato looked at me impassively. He was a man who knew when to hold his tongue.

"Okay, Mr. Sato. I'm in."

#

CHAPTER 3

The next week was one long funeral. There was no official announcement of casualty figures, but it was thought somewhere in the range of three to four thousand were killed or injured.

The whole city was somber and still. The store windows were taped up, some in elaborate patterns. Outside May's Market, shoppers waited quietly in line, allowed in one-by-one when someone left the store. Downtown buildings were sandbagged, with armed guards at the more important ones. Stores began to close by 3:30. Hundreds had simply never reopened.

Every man, woman, and child above a certain age was ordered to get a gas mask, and required to carry it at all times, under penalty of fine and imprisonment. Scaffolding went up around Aloha Tower and they began to paint it in camouflage, which struck me as a colossal waste of good paint.

Tuesday morning, Sato's right-hand man, George Koga, called me at my office and asked to meet me at Triangle Park. When I got there, I could see the park was carefully chosen —small enough to go unguarded, but large enough to permit private conversation. The park was not far from the main train station, which meant there were enough people milling around that Koga and I didn't stand out.

This close to the harbor, there was still a scent of death in the air, mixed with tar and burnt fuel oil. We each took a seat on a park bench and lit a cigarette against the stench. After the briefest of pleasantries, Koga got right down to business.

"How familiar are you, Mr. Ross, with Japanese funeral customs?"

"Not very. I know it is a rather elaborate process, with lots of specific steps that must be taken. I've been to Japanese wakes and funerals—well not a wake exactly."

Koga smiled. "There is no reason you should know our ways, sir. And I call them 'wakes' all the time. But allow me to further enlighten you, if you will, on the subject. Thanks to you, the family has been able to perform the first formal step. In Japanese we call it *matsugo no mizu*, which is to say, 'washing of the lips.' It is the deceased's last taste of water before undertaking the transition. The entire process of bereavement cannot begin until the first step is complete. So, we have you to thank for that. The rest, as you suggest, is quite complex. The more cynical among us might even say it was designed to ensure plenty of lucrative work for the priestly class—both Shinto and Buddhist, mind you, so everyone's bread gets buttered.

"Here is why all of this matters. You must not interview Daniel's family, or even his friends, until after the wake, the funeral, and the reception that follows. I would also recommend, by the way, that you attend each of these events yourself."

"Of course," I said, trying to sound as if I had known it all along.

"Ordinarily, the wake would be held in the evening hours, but owing to the blackout, it will be this afternoon at three o'clock. Unfortunately, the Nakajima's home isn't large enough to accommodate the anticipated number of mourners, so it will be held at Hosoi Chapel, though this fact troubles Mr. Nakajima greatly. He is, you see, a very traditional man."

"I understand."

"In the meantime," Koga said, "there is one thing you can be doing. In the week before he was murdered, Daniel was on Kauai, taking care of a sick uncle. While he was there, he wrote letters—one each day, I'm told—to his girlfriend. I expect to have those letters later today, and I will see to it they are delivered to your office."

"That's great," I said. "I'd like to get started right away. Can we get in touch with the uncle, at the appropriate time?"

"Ah, in that regard we are one step ahead of you, Mr. Ross. I've sent a cable to the uncle, expressing condolences, of course. It may stretch propriety a bit, but I told him to expect our call next week. We have the telephone number for the plantation office."

"When *is* it okay to proceed? With the interviews of family and friends."

"I would recommend any time after the seventh day following the death. There are rituals that must be performed on days three, seven, and forty-nine. And for the first week or so, there is a period of deep mourning that is not to be disturbed. So, say the fifteenth? I will make arrangements for you to see Daniel's parents, girlfriend, and closest friends. Is there any particular order in which you wish to interview them?"

I thought for a moment. "Yes, there is. I would like to speak with the friends first. They might tell me something useful for when I question the parents and the girlfriend."

Koga slid a card across the bench. It had two sets of numbers on it. He pointed to the first number.

"This number is answered at all times. Just say who you are and with whom you wish to speak, presumably me. If, for any reason, you require immediate assistance, ring the second number. Identify yourself and state your location. Please memorize the numbers."

He pulled an envelope from his pocket. "This is a letter of introduction, written in English and Japanese and signed by Sato-san. It will get you into places that might otherwise be closed to you. It might even get you out of a certain amount of trouble, but there are, naturally, no guarantees."

"Naturally," I said.

"Something else to keep in mind, Mr. Ross: there may be times when it is unwise to trust the telephones, especially in the atmosphere currently prevailing. A message left at the counter of China Luck Cleaners, downtown, and addressed to Dr. Quong, will be delivered to me within the hour. Any questions, Mr. Ross?"

"*China* Luck?"

Koga smiled his best Chamber of Commerce smile. "You have many unseen allies, Mr. Ross."

"That's comforting to know," I said.

"Just don't get too comfortable. I have accomplished a thing or two in this life. I consider myself a capable man, from a long line of capable men. And women for that matter. My grandmother twelve generations back was a samurai. Even still, I do not envy you your task."

"Your *grandmother*?"

Koga smiled. "She fought at the Battle of Senbon Matsubara, in 1580, and lived to tell about it. Had she not, I would not be sitting in this park, enjoying a visit with you, sir. We have had many celebrated female samurai. That's one of the many things you westerners do not know about us. But don't be too impressed. We samurai started out as poet warriors and ended up, at least on the home islands, as a bunch of sycophants and bureaucrats, most of whom went to their death beds without once having tasted warfare."

"Isn't that always the way it goes?" I asked.

Kogo gave me a knowing look, rose, and offered his hand.

"Good luck to you, sir," he said with an almost undetectable note of warning not to screw things up.

#

Memorizing the phone numbers was no great feat. They were four digits each, which meant they were among the earliest telephones installed on the island. I tore up the pieces and put them in three separate trash bins, as I walked up Hotel Street toward The Bronx. For reasons I couldn't quite put my finger on, I needed to see how Nalani was doing. Behind me, the train sounded its whistle and pulled slowly out of the station on its daily route to Kaena Point, Kahuka, and Wailaua. It would come back to town laden with pineapple, and sugar, and cattle—good news for everyone lined up to get in May's Market.

Everywhere I looked there were "Closed until further

notice" signs and black wreaths on shop doors. Dr. Hashimoto's Scientific Massage; Mishima Fancy Ladies' Dresses; the Muriyama Brothers, painters and decorators. All were closed tight to show *mahalo* for the fallen. Akahoshi Drugs, however, was opened, so I stepped in and called Tommy Ford from one of the phone booths in the back. With so little to be done on the Nakajima case until after the funeral, I wanted to see if he would give me a peek at the Heston murder file.

The sergeant said Tommy was "out rounding up some more Japs," so I left a message for him to call me at my office.

The Bronx was still very much a hospital ward for the less severely injured cases who were not yet ambulatory. I was barely in the door before Vassar collared me. Her olive skin glowed with excitement, her brown eyes wide.

"Sit down, Mac," she said, falling into the chair across from me and putting her cowboy boots on the coffee table between us, one ankle over the other. "I need your help."

"My help?"

"Have you ever heard of Chief Michaels Ten Commandments?"

"Sure, that's the rules of the road for what you can and cannot do as it relates to the brothel business in Honolulu."

"Yeah, well, first of all there are thirteen, okay? But the good news is there's a new sheriff in town. We're under martial law now, right? So, I figure when we open back up in a few days, maybe a couple of weeks from now, tops, old Chief Michaels won't be in charge anymore, right?"

"Well, I wouldn't—"

"Here's the deal. We're willing to keep the *business* in the business district. But we want to live *where* and *how* we want to —almost like we were real people. Is that so crazy? I'm telling you all this because, when the time comes, we might need your help launching a trial balloon or two with the Army brass. Best I can tell you know everybody on the island, Mac."

"That sounds like a cause I can get behind."

"Thanks, Mac, you're a swell guy." It was the second time

in a week someone had told me I was a swell guy. It made me feel good inside. Maybe I was getting soft in my old age.

"Glad to be of help. Have you seen Nalani today?"

"Last I heard, she was at Schofield, interviewing for some kind of clerical job. Looks like she's going straight on us, Mac." She grinned. "I hope you won't look down on her for it."

"Well, it is scandalous, to be sure. And a demotion to go from The Bronx to the Army, of all places. But, so long as she's discreet about it, I guess it's okay. Say, have you ever thought about running for Mayor?"

She pulled the boots back down onto the carpet and bounced up out of the chair. "No, I have enough pricks to deal with as it is."

#

At my office there was a large envelope under the door. Sato's office was the return address. It had been opened. Written in block capitals on the back: WE HAVE THE LETTERS. YOU WON'T BE NEEDING THEM. THIS WILL BE YOUR ONLY WARNING. RESIGN THE NAKAJIMA CASE. –A FRIEND.

A friend. That's how the last anonymous letter had been signed. But they couldn't possibly come from the same source. I lit a cigarette, looked up Sato's office in the telephone book and dialed it. It seemed silly to call the special number for this. The prim secretary answered and got Koga on the line. I told him the news. He didn't seem overly concerned. Most clients would have panicked, but then George Koga and Kintaro Sato were unlike any clients I'd ever had.

Koga said, "Naturally, we took the precaution of making copies. I'll send someone over now with another set. Stay there, if you don't mind, until they reach you."

Ten minutes later, there was a knock at the outer office door. One of the mahjong players bowed and handed me an envelope without a word. I could tell he still had his heater, even though Japanese residents had been instructed to turn in all weapons and radios. He must be *nisei*, hence an American citizen, or have some special dispensation. I bowed in return, and he walked briskly away. Just another day at the office for one who does the bidding of Sato-san.

I made sure to lock the outer door and turn the lights off there. In my office, I poured a drink and began to read letters written by a dead man to his girlfriend.

December 1, 1941
Kukuiolono Camp, Eleele, Kauai
Dear Keiko,

Thank you for your letter. It was waiting for me when I finally got here tonight, and it lifted my spirits after a rough day. I'm not much for sea travel, even if it's only a few hours between the islands. From your first words, I felt better, because you addressed me as "My Dearest Man."

I miss you already. If we have to be apart, I wish I was at least at home, where I could listen to *Night, Night* on the phonograph and think of you. As it is, I'm at a smelly old work camp, with no record player, and no electricity even.

My uncle said he felt better just knowing I was here, though. I'm going to take turns watching him tonight with his oldest friend in the world, who isn't much younger (or healthier) than he is. At the moment, uncle's fever is down, but you know how that goes. He seems to have really gone downhill since my aunt died.

Anyway, I'd better get to sleep. I will mail this tomorrow, when I take uncle to the doctor in Lihue.
Yours 'til,
Daniel

The next was dated, December 2.
Dear Keiko,

Every time I write your name, I am reminded it means "blessed child," which makes good sense to me because you sure are a blessing. Since the day we met, the world has felt like a new and better place to me.

Today was a long, busy one. I got up early and made breakfast and looked around the place. I had forgotten how rustic it is. Picture little wooden houses clustered around an open area, with corrugated roofs that are starting to rust, and little outhouses in the back of each house. Every house has its own soaking tub, which is the only place to take a bath.

I thank God I don't have to live the way my uncle and his friend have all these many years. I confess, I like the modern conveniences of life. Aren't you glad you're not going steady with some guy who has to work on a plantation on Kauai? Something tells me by the time the week is out, I won't be taking my little place in Honolulu for granted so much.

I do enjoy walking down to the beach for a morning swim. I can't do that every day on Oahu. It sure beats the soaking tub! After the swim, I took my uncle into town. He and the plantation supervisor are old friends. They were even in each other's weddings, all those years ago! So, he let me borrow the plantation's truck. I ground a few gears, but in no time, I was doing pretty okay.

The doctor said it's a bronchial infection. I may not be spelling that right, so please forgive me. Don't get out your English teacher's red pencil and mark me down if I didn't get it right, without a dictionary to look it up in. He gave uncle some pills and a cough syrup that smells like it's mostly alcohol.

There wasn't a soul in Lihue that I knew from all those summers I spent working here, which made the place feel odd to me. Just a bunch of strangers in an otherwise familiar place.

Speaking of strangers, my friend Hatsuno is due back in Honolulu this week. He just finished his masters at Columbia University in New York City. He's a really good guy and I know that you two would like each other. He's going to teach math at Central Intermediate starting in the spring, so if you see him out and about at any of our usual haunts, please introduce yourself. Don't worry, I won't be jealous!

It's so funny, but while I was at the doctor's office today, I happened to hear *These Things I Love,* and so, of course, I thought of you. That's the number one tune on my personal Hit Parade, and I think you know why.

Yours 'til,

Daniel

Over the course of the next few days, Daniel continued to write Keiko. It was heartbreaking stuff. But there was nothing remotely useful that I could see. His time seemed to be taken up with morning swims, nursing his uncle, and trying to do things around the house that would be helpful after he was gone.

He apparently had remarkably little contact with anyone other than his uncle and the plantation supervisor. In one letter, he reported being invited to a "rum party," but ended up not going. In another, he commented on Keiko's plan to work for Island Real Estate over her summer recess. "You'll be a regular Kitty Foyle," he wrote, referencing the Ginger Rogers movie that was all the rave.

In the last letter, dated December 4, he told Keiko he would call and walk over to see her as soon as he got home. He also said his time at the plantation had made him reflect on what it meant to be *nisei* in Hawaii.

"Sometimes, I feel like I'm two people. Daniel and Hideo (like my middle name). One of us, Hideo, is quiet and dutiful to his family and the traditions that mean so much to them. But Daniel is expected to be an independent and adventurous American. It's hard being two people!"

The letters left me no more enlightened, but in a decidedly somber mood, which was just as well since it was nearly time for the wake. Now, at least, I had a better sense of the man I was going to mourn and whose murder I was expected to solve. I put the letters back in the envelope and into the file labelled

NAKAJIMA, then into the safe. I wasn't about to lose them a second time.

#

I was putting on my black suit when the phone rang.

"Mac Ross, Investigations."

It was Tommy Ford, sounding tired. "Hey, Mac. Got your message. Just got back in the office. How goes it?"

"Well, it's only Tuesday but I've already had my first threatening letter of the week if that tells you anything. I seem to be everyone's favorite correspondent all of a sudden. Thanks for returning my call, partner. Listen, I found out this morning I can't interview anyone on the Nakajima case until early next week, and I was wondering if you would make me a copy of the Heston file. It would give me something to do in the blackout besides being lonely and far too close to sober. I'm on half rations with the whiskey, which is running out fast. Might keep me off the streets. Or out of the psych ward, more like it."

Tommy laughed. "Yeah, I'm in the same boat. No word yet on when the liquor stores are going to reopen, or the bars can serve anything stronger than beer. So, you're determined to work on the Nakajima thing?"

I found myself telling Tommy Ford what I had told Marcia. "It's what I do."

He paused. "Sure, I can get you a copy. We've got volunteers out the ying over here after they made that announcement on the radio. It would be good to give them something that wasn't purely make-work. Do you need copies of the crime scene photographs?"

"Not really. I've seen them. Can't *unsee* them, for that matter. Photostats are fine. And throw in the Nakajima file, what there is so far, if you would."

"Won't be much on Nakajima."

"I understand. Maybe a crime scene report, though, right?"

"How does tomorrow at noon sound?"

"Sounds like you're bucking for HPD employee of the

month."

"Screw that," he said and hung up.

#

On the way to the wake on Kukui Street, I swung by The Bronx and left a message asking Nalani to call me. Mr. Koga was waiting for me outside Hosoi Chapel. He shook my hand, then placed an envelope in it.

"This is a *koden*. It is a gift of money for the family. It is customary for friends and associates of the deceased to provide one, to assist the family with the rather significant expense of all that buttered bread we talked about. I would be grateful if you would present it to them. I have one as well, of course, but Mr. Sato does not want to be seen as being ostentatious. It wouldn't do."

"Oh, I'm sorry, I—"

"You'll be doing me a favor. Listen, once we are inside, there will be little opportunity to talk. Were the letters of any use?"

I knew Koga had copies of the letters, so he most certainly had read them.

"I'm afraid not."

Koga gave me a curt nod that said his question was mostly a matter of form and gestured toward the door of the funeral home.

Inside, I recognized a few of the heavy-weight Japanese businessmen who must have come out of respect for Keiko's family. A steady parade of men in well-tailored suits came by to greet Sato and engage him in brief, whispered conversation. I recognized the chairman of Sumitomo Bank among them. I also noticed that Sato's trinity of bodyguards were never far away. Apparently mah jong wasn't their only skill. Around the room, there were several *nisei* of Daniel's age, a few *haoles*, and a Filipino woman. I suspected they were Daniel's colleagues.

The rituals were performed by a Shinto priest, entirely in Japanese. I understood almost none of it, but it struck me how alike the many nations are when it comes to the rituals of death. I didn't understand the meaning of the words, but the tone of respect and veneration was thoroughly familiar.

Near the end, the priest turned and faced the coffin as if to speak directly to the spirit of the deceased. He bowed especially deeply, and began to chant in a sonorous, hieratical voice. If only he could ask the dead man's spirit who had put a bullet through his head.

After the service, the ever-popular twelfth step was performed, known as *settai*—refreshments. It was easy enough to see why the *koden* was a useful custom. The catered food was beyond sumptuous. And we hadn't even made it to the funeral yet. After expressing my condolences to the family and presenting my little packet of money, I tried hovering around the various groups, but the teachers were the only ones speaking English. I listened to them reminisce about the things they had done with their friend, now taken from them. When my heart couldn't take it anymore, I found Koga, said goodbye, and headed for the exit to beat the curfew.

#

At the house on Paki Avenue, the sun dipped quickly toward the horizon, as it had Saturday night. But only the sun and Diamond Head were the same. The park looked like an overused cantonment. There were giant, muddy ruts in the grass where half-tracks had been driven back and forth. Aerials were strung between the taller palms. I wondered what the zoo animals made of it all.

The phone was ringing as I came in the door.

"Hello."

It was Nalani. "Hello, Mac."

"Hey, I've been trying to track you down all day."

"Well, I'm a busy woman. After all, you're talking to the administrative assistant to the deputy commander of the 24th Infantry Division."

"Really? That's fabulous. Congratulations!"

"Thank you. You didn't think I would be a working girl forever, did you? I promised myself I would save enough to take care of my mother, then get a real job. I have and I did."

"You amaze me."

"Thank you, Mac. I admit, I am proud of myself."

"As well you should be. Listen, I'd like to ask you to dinner, sort of start this whole thing over, if we can. But there is no dinner to ask you to at the moment, with the curfew. So, how would lunch do?"

"Ah, that's sweet. I'd like to. Yes. But my first day off is the Sunday before Christmas."

"Ouch. I have to wait almost two weeks to see you?"

"I'm afraid so, Mac. Duty calls. Sorry."

"It's not your fault. Okay, how about the restaurant at the Moana Hotel on, what is that—the twenty-first? Say, noon?"

"Perfect. I'll see you then."

"Wait, I don't even have the phone number at your mother's house."

An instant of silence. Then, she said, "You want to start over, right?"

"Yes."

"Well, if you're a nice, proper gentleman at lunch, we'll see."

"That *is* starting over."

"It was your idea," she said brightly.

"Fair enough."

#

The next morning, I bought a paper from the newsy outside my office building and read the front page while I waited on the elevator to creep down four floors and back up. I couldn't help noticing that our elevator didn't smell as good as Sato's. The standing joke among us tenants in the den of thieves was that the elevator was an OTIS, which could only stand for "Oh, This Is Slow." It wasn't much in the way of elevator humor, but it was always greeted with far more laughter than it deserved.

The newspaper headlines were less sensational. Word had it that the grand poohbahs in the Army and Navy command had come down hard on the *Star-Bulletin* for their "Saboteurs Land Here" headline the day after the attack. The words "aid and comfort to the enemy" were said to have been bandied about, which is tantamount to treason—a hanging offense. The chilling effect was evident. Suddenly, the paper was all about practical matters and official pronouncements. A summary of the myriad regulations already put into effect by decree of the foresightful military government; where and when to pick up your gas mask; how to get ready for the enumeration.

The elevator groaned, as I stepped off. Nearing my office, I realized someone was inside. My guns were all locked up at the house and the shack, or in the inner office safe. But I took a chance and opened the door quickly, slamming it shut behind me for effect.

A young Hawaiian woman was bent over the typewriter, a letter opener in her hand, fiddling with the ribbon. She jumped and screamed. Or, screamed and jumped. It was a photo finish.

"Mr. Ross! You scared the hell out of me. Excuse me for saying so."

"That makes us even. Who are you?"

"I'm Lina Kaimana," she said, as if I should have known the answer. "Tommy Ford, at HPD, sent me. Tommy says you need a new assistant. So, here I am, boss!"

"He may have said I *need* a new assistant, but did he fail to mention I'm not *looking* for a new assistant?"

"I don't understand. If you need, you need. So, of course you *look*. But now you won't have to, see? I'm very good, Mr. Ross. I used to work for the big boss at Hawaiian Trust," she said, then with a frown, "That is until his wife made him fire me." She seemed sure this fact would seal the deal.

"Tell me your name again."

"You may call me Miss Kaimana," she said, placing special emphasis on the *Miss*. "It means 'power of the sea,' in Hawaiian,

46

but then you probably knew that. Tommy says you've gone native."

"Tommy says a lot of things. But you see, Miss Kaimana, I don't want anything to do with the power of the sea. The power of the sea frightens me. I can't swim."

She looked puzzled. "You live on Oahu, and you can't swim?"

"Never got around to it."

Her expression telegraphed that she was suddenly unsure what she had gotten herself into. "But Tommy says you are big surfer kind of guy. How can you surf but not swim?"

I smiled. "Can you think of a faster way to become good at surfing than not being able to swim? It's why I never fall off the board."

Her face worked its way through successive expressions, as her mind processed the information, ending in another broad smile.

"You're pulling my leg. Anyways, boss, you had two calls. One from a man who wouldn't give his name or leave a message and believe me I tried. The other from a Mrs. Martin. She says her husband, who is in the army, has been unfaithful to her," here she pulled another frown that slowly evolved back to a smile as she read her notes. "But she says if you can catch the bastard red-handed, she will make it worth your while."

"Does she know how much my while is worth?"

Miss Kaimana glanced around the office, making an instant appraisal of the value of my while. The look she shot back suggested it didn't add up to much. But, in the next instant, she reminded herself of her own need for gainful employment.

"She sounds very wealthy over the phone, boss. She has one of those rich voices; she can afford us. When should I schedule her?"

I sighed. It would be nice to have an assistant again. I worked best when I had a certain level of organization in my life. Within reason. And it made sense to have someone in the office when I couldn't be there. The letters from Sato demonstrated that well enough.

Miss Kaimana sensed my weakness and moved in for the kill with the ruthlessness of a pit viper.

"I can type sixty words per minutes, boss. And take Gregg shorthand at two hundred." With a wide smile she pointed to the wall, where she had already hung her official Gregg Shorthand Certificate, her Honolulu School of Business diploma, and another fancy sheepskin for something called The Palmer Method.

A wise man knows defeat when he sees it staring him in the face. "Alright, but I can only afford to pay you $40 a week. That's at the high end of the going rate."

"Did I mention that I know double-entry bookkeeping, boss?"

"Okay, $45, but that's my limit, Miss Kaimana." I instantly rationalized that it would actually save me a fair amount with the accountants if she could do the basic bookkeeping and let them file the returns.

"Dear boss," she said, coming quickly around the desk. In rapid succession, she pumped my hand, kissed my cheek, gave me the briefest of hugs, and went back around her desk. "Anyways, what about Mrs. Martin?"

I fought off the impulse to fire her. "Let's put her off until next week. Say, Wednesday,"

She clicked her teeth. "She might choose to go elsewhere."

"I hope she does," I said, heading into my office. "Hold my calls, please." I really didn't expect or even mind any calls; it just felt good to be able to say it again. "Oh, and Miss Kaimana?"

"Yes, boss."

"Look up Sterling Signs in the book and have them scrape and repaint the outer door to read, 'Mac Ross, Confidential Investigations.' Got it?"

She scribbled rapidly on her notepad. "Got it, boss."

"And don't call me boss."

#

CHAPTER 4

December 15 came at last. Koga had arranged for me to interview Daniel Nakajima's friends and colleagues at a location familiar to everyone: the Nuuanu YMCA. In the gym, I recognized Billy Bongo and the Club Nisei Orchestra, likely rehearsing for the first War Bond Drive Concert—an upcoming city-wide battle of the bands hastily arranged to raise money for the war effort.

Billy's clear tenor and the band's uniformly good musicianship made them serious contenders, if the atmosphere of the moment would allow. His vocals reverberated off the empty space, providing an eerie echo, as he sang *Gomen Nasai* —"I'm Sorry," a *nisei* hit. The lyrics implore a young woman to forgive and forget and be sweethearts once more.

In the back of the room, a group of young teachers stood awkwardly, waiting for me to interview them. You had to look no farther than their fashion choices, adopted long ago, to see where their allegiance lay as between Japan and the U.S. The young women wore pleated skirts and saddle oxfords; the men were in corduroy pants and Argyle sweaters.

I spent a couple of hours questioning them. It was time well spent, providing a much fuller picture of the victim, not to mention a satisfying sense that I was finally getting into the traces with this case. My report:

On Monday, December 15, 1941, I interviewed the following friends and colleagues of VICTIM DANIEL NAKAJIMA:

DAVID MAHUKA, 24, male, Teacher
QUAN PUNG YUEN, 26, male, Teacher
BETTY HUNEA, 24, female, Teacher
HELEN AGUIAR, 25, female, Teacher
TOKITCHI KURASHITA, 23, male, student at UofH

SUMMARY OF FINDINGS:

VICTIM DANIEL NAKAJIMA was both well-known and well-liked by the interview subjects, all but one of whom are teachers at Central Intermediate School, where VICTIM taught fifth grade (and previously twelfth grade) history. They reported that teachers at the school tend to socialize almost exclusively with each other. The interview subjects reported he or she has, at various times, gone to movies, dances, concerts, "wee golf" outings, and other social gatherings with VICTIM.

For the last year or so, the girlfriend of the VICTIM, KEIKO MATSUMO, a sixth grade English teacher at the school, joined VICTIM and the subjects on many such outings. The couple were said to get along well with each other and were generally believed to be ideally suited.

Said AGUIAR: "They were just like Cary Grant and Audrey Hepburn in *Holiday*. They were meant for each other." Miss AGUIAR said that, like the couple in the film, VICTIM and KEIKO MATSUMO came from different economic backgrounds, but "it never seemed to hinder their relationship or their regard for one another."

None of the subjects interviewed could imagine VICTIM having any enemies, with one clear exception: DAICHI HATTORI, the former boyfriend or steady date (descriptions were mixed) of KEIKO MATSUMO. HATTORI is said to have been jealous of any attention paid KEIKO by any male, and to be bitter at what he was said to call their "breakup." HUNEA insisted that KEIKO MATSUMO and HATTORI were "never boyfriend and girlfriend."

All interviewees said that, if they were asked to name possible suspects, HATTORI would be the only name on their list. Several interviewees made mention of HATTORI's perceived poor manners and said this factor alone was enough to ensure he did not fit in well with their social group.

YUEN said he had heard rumors that HATTORI had some sort of "run-in with the law," though he was quick to add that he was personally unaware of any evidence to support the claim.

Only one subject, KURASHITA, had any first-hand knowledge of VICTIM's relationship with his family. KURASHITA described VICTIM as a dutiful son who gladly did everything he could to help his parents and his uncle.

All but one of the subjects, YUEN, had foreknowledge of VICTIM's trip to Kauai to assist his uncle. None reported having had communication with VICTIM during the period from his departure until his subsequent death.

No deception was detected. There was no attempt to evade questions, to provide vague or short answers, and no conflicting information.

All interviewees provided local contact information and expressed a strong willingness to answer any follow-up questions, or otherwise assist the investigation into VICTIM's death.

\#

From the YMCA, I made the short trip to the murder scene, not because I expected to uncover anything of evidentiary value, but because I wanted to see the lay of the land for myself, prior to reading the crime scene report I hoped would be forthcoming from Tommy Ford. It would have taken me only about two minutes to get there, if I didn't have to cross one of the busiest roads on Oahu.

Daniel had been walking, at or just after midnight, having arrived late from Kauai. Not far from his apartment, he walked past a line of gnarled wiliwili trees. The most likely scenario in my mind was that someone had hidden behind the third tree in the line, waiting until just the moment Daniel passed, stepped out quickly, and shot him in the back of the head. There were no surviving signs of a struggle, though the crime scene report would, I hoped, give me details. There were, however, three bouquets—all of white chrysanthemums—lying on the spot where Daniel fell.

The most telling aspect, to me, was that nothing about the scene, or the wound for that matter, suggested it was a robbery gone bad. Shooting someone in the back of the head is an intensely personal and intimate act. Either the shooter had a beef with the victim, or he (or she) was a professional, hell-bent on making sure it was one shot and done. Or, conceivably, both. Homicides arising from a robbery tend to end with randomly placed shots to the anterior of the body. This was execution style, pure and simple.

When Daniel had failed to arrive at Keiko's house after forty-five minutes, and when repeated calls to Daniel's apartment went unanswered, Keiko called the police, who responded immediately, traced the only possible route a pedestrian would take from his apartment to her house, and found the body.

The white chrysanthemums were an ambiguous presence. If Daniel had been killed over some issue of bushido honor, it would be expected that he would be shot in the head, if not actually decapitated. And, in such a case, chrysanthemums would be nothing more than a calling card. A warning to the next poor bastard who might consider crossing them, though I found it hard to square a gangland hit with the wholesome image of Daniel.

#

Back at my office, I put my feet up on the desk, buzzed Miss Kaimana on the intercom, and asked her to get Marcia Heston on the line. It made me feel expansive and important to have help around the place again.

"Oh, is that—"

"Yes, she was married to Hes."

"Well, I won't mention the door, then," she said.

I tried to imagine in what circumstance mentioning the door would be appropriate but got nowhere before her eager voice came through the speaker.

"Mrs. Heston on line one." Not bad. Maybe Mr. Hawaiian Trust's wife had been wrong about Miss K.

"Marcia, how are you?"

"You have a new secretary. I bet she's a dish."

"No, no. Tommy Ford sent her over. I owe him so many favors, it was impossible to tell her no."

"What does that have to do with her being a dish?" she asked, with a throaty laugh. Marcia had a long and storied career as a matchmaker.

"Nothing, she's just not my type."

"Give it a chance. You might be surprised. But you didn't call me to talk about your new secretary, or your love life."

"You're right. My love life is stuck in neutral at the moment. Not worth talking about. I'm just following up on that card you were going to drop by—the detective from San Francisco."

"Oh, my lands. I forgot all about that. I'm sorry, Mac. I really am. Can I get it to you tomorrow? I've been volunteering at Queen's Hospital. We got all the overflow from Pearl and

Schofield. It's the most difficult and yet the most fulfilling thing I've done in I don't know when. Maybe ever. I feel as if I've come back from the dead."

"Welcome back."

"Thanks, Mac."

"I would ask you about *your* new friend, the colonel, but it wouldn't seem fair, since we're not talking about our love lives."

"To tell you the truth, I've only seen him once in the last week, and that was to drop off a casserole." She laughed. "I bet you never thought you would hear me utter those words—drop off a casserole."

"We live in interesting times, Marcia."

"That we do."

"Take care of yourself. Let me know if I can be of any help."

"I will. I'll get by tomorrow, I swear."

Miss Kaimana must have been listening closely because the instant I hung up the phone she tapped on my door. She came in with an expectant look and an Air Mail envelope. It was from my man in San Francisco.

"Well, aren't you going to open it, boss?"

I slit open the envelope and read the letter.

"Dear Mac: Not a lot to report. I'm still working on recruiting someone on the inside at Hibernia Bank to see what we can find out about the account Hes wired a quarter million dollars to. You know how that goes. Hard to say when we might hit pay dirt. I'll keep you posted, Max."

Drawing a clear conclusion form the look on my face, Miss Kaimana went back to her desk, clearly disappointed in me and my man in Frisco. I thought about updating Koga, then realized I really didn't have anything that could be called an update.

#

I had just enough time to get to my interview with Daniel Nakajima's girlfriend. Traffic had become a nightmare since the curfew eliminated so many hours out of every day. As I crept along, I kept looking at my watch and tapping the handlebars.

Meanwhile, just to torment myself, my mind turned over and over the many questions I couldn't answer, like 'who sent the anonymous letter,' and 'who stole the first set of love letters Daniel wrote Keiko?'

At Central Intermediate School, I could tell from the parking lot the place had been thoroughly taken over by the Army. That explained why my instructions were to meet Keiko Matsumo in the basement.

Every school in the Territory had been closed since the attack, but teachers were training to conduct the enumeration. It was thought that registering everyone and issuing identity cards would make it more difficult for Japan to land agents intending to blend into the populace, but some said it was just so the bodies would be easier to identify after the next air raid. Ironically, it was *nisei* who would be doing the lion's share of the enumerating, since so many of them were teachers.

Miss Matsumo met me at the door and escorted me through the busy corridors and down to the basement where she had arranged for us to use the building superintendent's tiny office. It had the schoolhouse smell of floor wax, disinfectant, and slow drains.

Keiko wore a simple black knit dress with a scalloped neckline that showed her sinuous neck and chiseled jaw to good effect. Two small freckles were aligned like Castor and Pollux, above and below her collarbone. Her chestnut hair was parted slightly off-center, bangs falling asymmetrically to just along the top of strong eyebrows perched above almond-shaped eyes. Even in her grief, she was a lovely young woman. She settled in behind the small, cluttered desk.

"Again, I'm so sorry for your loss, Miss Matsumo."

"Thank you, Mr. Ross."

"I know it might seem early for me to call on you, asking a bunch of questions, but we need all the help we can get if we are to investigate Daniel's murder properly.

"Of course. I'll do anything to help."

For the next hour, Keiko told me about first her friendship

and then her romance with Daniel Nakajima. It was clear from her answers they had been deeply in love. She painted a picture of a typical young American couple, enjoying their time together —doing lesson plans, playing badminton or miniature golf, going to the movies. Only one cloud darkened the picture, Daichi Hattori.

"Tell me about your relationship with your former boyfriend, Mr. Hattori."

She frowned deeply. "He was never my boyfriend," she said, in a dismissive tone. "We went out a few times, that's all."

"I see. Is it possible Mr. Hattori considered himself your boyfriend?"

For the first time in our conversation, her voice reflected her privileged upbringing.

"It doesn't matter what he considered himself, Mr. Ross. I told him I was in love with Daniel."

"When was that?"

"Months ago."

"How did he take it?"

"Not well at all. I expected he might make a fuss, so I chose a public place to tell him."

"What, exactly, was his reaction?"

"Oh, he made quite a scene. Cursed me, called me all sorts of bad names and stormed off. I was horrified and humiliated, but it was worth it to be rid of him."

"Did you hear from him after that?"

"Yes. Well, he sent me notes. The first one began with an apologetic tone, lots of remorse. But by the end of the note, it was half threat and half plea. After that, I never opened them."

"Do you still have these notes?"

"No, I threw them away as soon as I received them."

"How many would you say there were?"

"Half a dozen, I suppose."

"Miss Matsumo, is Mr. Hattori a violent person?"

"I've never known him to be. After we quit going out, I heard all sorts of things. That he had been in a knife fight once.

Something vague about being in trouble with the police. I didn't know what to believe. I just wanted to move on."

"Of course. Would you say it's possible Mr. Hattori was so distraught over your relationship with Daniel that he killed him?"

"Daichi is impulsive. Prone to anger. He once told me, how did he put it, that his logic switches off and his rage takes over. But he was always contrite after. I find it hard to imagine he would kill someone."

"Is there any way Hattori could have known Daniel would be walking along School Street from his apartment to your house at midnight that night?"

It was clear she had already asked herself the question. "That's the part that makes no sense, Mr. Ross. I don't see how he could have. The boat from Kauai ran late. Daniel should have been back around nine, and I expected him to call me and come right over. He had told me he would, in his last letter. So, I don't see how Daichi—or anyone—could have known he would be there around midnight. It seems highly unlikely. Although I suppose he could have just happened to run into Daniel."

I nodded. "Do you know where I might find the letters you wrote Daniel while he was taking care of his uncle?"

"I assume they would be at his apartment. He liked to keep our letters. He said one of the things he liked most about me was my way with the English language. I'm an English teacher, you know."

"Yes, Ma'am. I expect to be able to look around Daniel's apartment tomorrow or the next day. If I find them, I will see that you get them. And I would like to read them, with your permission, of course."

"I would very much like to have them and you are welcome to read them if you think it might help."

"Is there anything you would like to add? Any question I didn't ask you that I should have asked?"

"There is one thing I think you should know, Mr. Ross. I don't know that it makes any difference, but Daniel and I were secretly engaged to be married. We couldn't really tell anyone, until we had told our parents and received their blessing, but the plan was for Daniel to ask my father for my hand as soon as he got back from Kauai."

"Did either of you tell anyone about your engagement? Could word have gotten back to Mr. Hattori?"

"I told only my dearest friend, Betty Hunea. I believe you have already spoken to her. She swears she told no one, and I believe her, for what that's worth. As for Daniel, I can't imagine him telling anyone except perhaps his uncle. Daniel and his uncle were very close. His uncle regarded Daniel as the leading light of the family—the one the entire previous generation sacrificed for. Bet on, one might say. It's possible he would tell his uncle, and swear him to secrecy, knowing the old man would have few people he could tell. Of course, you can ask Daniel's uncle."

"I have a call scheduled with him. Do you know him well?"

"Not at all, really, but our family is well known throughout the Territory," she said matter of factly. "It's possible his uncle might know my father, or of him at least, and that Daniel might let him in on the secret, knowing it would give a sick old man a moment of joy. That was Daniel to a tee." She flicked at the corner of one eye with a long, manicured finger.

"One last question. When Daniel called you that night, to say he was coming over, what were his exact words, do you recall?"

"He said something like, 'I'm so anxious to see you. I can't wait to tell you about my trip. I'll be there as fast as I can.'"

"Is that all?"

"He said he had finally seen a ghost at the plantation."

"A Ghost?"

"Yes. You see Daniel's uncle has told him stories for years about how he could see the ghosts of his ancestors around the plantation and in the fields. As a boy it scared Daniel, but as he got older, he realized it was his uncle's way of keeping Daniel on his best behavior on his summer visits. Except apparently on this trip he saw a ghost himself. He promised to tell me the whole story as soon as he got to my apartment."

"Is there anything else you can think of?"

"No, we hung up so he could start walking."

"You've been very helpful, Miss Matsumo." I wriggled out of the confined space and put a card in front of her. "If you think of anything else, anything at all, I would appreciate a call, however insignificant it might seem."

"I will. Thank you, Mr. Ross. Please find whoever did this to my Daniel." She dabbed at her eye.

"Don't worry, Miss Matsumo. We'll find them." I said it without thinking. It sounded hollow and unconvincing.

#

With petrol now rationed, I had the brilliant idea that as long as I was in the neighborhood, I should pick up my gas mask, since my designated distribution point happened to be on the ground floor of the school. The sergeant on duty was strangely chipper and good natured for someone who had to deal with members of the public for ten hours at a stretch. He had me fitted and checked out in no time. I signed a whole sheaf of papers, and I was the proud owner of one U.S. Navy Mark 1 Gas Mask, which looked suspiciously like a museum piece from the last war.

I made the mistake of asking, "What happens if there's actually a gas attack, Sergeant?"

"Well, if you're exposed to a nerve agent, someone is to come along and give you a thumping big shot of atropine. But whether they do or whether they don't, there's just two steps for you to remember."

"Really? Just two, eh?"

"Yes, sir. It's pretty simple." He smiled amiably. "Step one is bend over. Step two is kiss your ass goodbye."

#

When I left the school, clouds, dark at their bases, filled the sky. I put my mask in the saddlebag and rode to HPD headquarters for a look at Daichi Hattori's criminal record.

At the intersection of Beretania and Pensacola, I saw Ah Nam Ho directing traffic, in his olive drab uniform and white gloves. He was, quite literally, an island-wide attraction, known for his antic gestures and remarkable dance moves, all while directing traffic in a way that never allowed a snarl. Directing traffic, when it's done well, is one of those things that looks ridiculously easy, but turns out to be hard as hell to do without fouling it up.

Today, however, he was eerily sedate as he waved me through. My heart dropped a few inches at the sight of it. Some of the color went out of paradise. It was increasingly clear that we had passed through some sort of threshold, with dramatic differences in the "before," and "after" pictures. Some people withered, almost physically. Others bloomed, energized by the emergency.

At headquarters, Tommy Ford was nowhere to be seen, so I let myself into the records room on the third floor as if I owned the joint. The entire building was overrun by unfamiliar volunteers, including members of the San Jose State football squad, who had been in town to play the University of Hawaii when they were left stranded by the war.

I found a thin file on Hattori. One arrest in February of '39 for buying, selling, or receiving stolen property—a bicycle. Not exactly the picture of a criminal mastermind, let alone a cold-blooded killer, but one never knows. It was the kind of charge that tells you very little, although Hattori did plead guilty and paid a $200 fine—quite a sum for a schoolteacher. Except for the personal information, fingerprints and the like, that was the extent of the file.

I got the attention of one of the footballers who was waiting patiently to be of help.

"I need a photostat of this single page, please. I'll wait here."

"Yes, sir. Usually takes about two or three minutes for them to process it."

"No rush. Thank you. And thank you for your service. You guys are great to pitch in. It means a lot."

He beamed. "Yes, sir."

It couldn't have been more than four or five minutes before he was back with a triumphant air. The negative print was perfectly legible, the blacks swapped for the whites. I thanked him again and tried to tip him, but he refused the offer with an air of incorruptibility.

"Would you mind refiling the original for me?"

"No, sir. Not at all," he said with the confidence of someone who had done it dozens of times before.

The time had come to pay a visit to Mr. Hattori, since he was the closest thing I had to a suspect.

#

The address on file for Daichi Hattori was 699 Waipa Lane, in a middle-class neighborhood, an easy, ten-minute walk from where Daniel Nakajima had met his death. I knocked on the door, the way I had learned to do it in my decade in law enforcement. Firmly but politely.

It was a neat but simply constructed apartment building with two floors, comprising six units. A lanai ran along the right edge of the complex, toward the back of the building, where it wrapped around, providing outdoor space for everyone, while only covering two sides of the building. The position of the lanai wasn't chosen for the view, which was in the other direction, but to catch the trade winds.

After my second knock, I heard a quiet rustling from somewhere inside the apartment. I walked quietly to the right, and quickly down the lanai toward the back of the building, arriving in time to see a young man leaving through a back door. I was just quick enough that he would have to come through me to go down the back steps.

"Mr. Hattori?"

"Who are you? Leave me alone."

"I just need a few minutes of your time, Mr. Hattori."

"I said leave me alone," he said, hotly, "I mean it. Get out of my way, damnit."

I planted myself firmly between Hattori and the steps, but not so close he could knock me down them. By the time he charged me, we were within just a few feet of each other, so he didn't have enough room to gain much momentum. Still, he was coming as hard as he could.

I hesitated an instant, then as he approached, I stepped forward with my left foot, planting it firmly and transferring my weight. I hit him hard, the open palm of my right hand landing squarely on his solar plexus—just below the sternum and above the abdominal muscles. The trick is to keep your arm relaxed. You have to practice it, because the instinct is to stiffen every muscle. Relaxing makes it quicker, and the shifting weight provides all the force you need, especially if your opponent is moving toward you.

The air left Hattori's lungs with an explosive rush, as his diaphragm did all of the work for me. He sat down heavily, shaking the deck timbers, a look of utter shock on his face.

While he gasped for breath, I grabbed his right ear, brought him to a near-standing position, and slung him sideways into a lawn chair, which skidded backward across the lanai. I pulled a second chair over until it was nearly on top of his toes and sat down on the edge of it.

"What do you say we try this again, Mr. Hattori?"

He was still struggling for breath, but he shook his head emphatically 'yes.'

"Do you have any weapon on you of any kind?"

His head signaled 'no.' He was getting a few sips of air now and color slowly returned to his face. I flashed my P.I. license.

I spoke calmly, as if he had answered my first knock and we were meeting one another for the first time. "Mr. Hattori, my name is Mac Ross. I'm a detective, working with HPD and the military government." It was something of a stretch, but there was just enough truth in it, in case I was ever called on it. "I'm investigating a murder that took place near here. Do you mind taking a few minutes to answer some questions for me?"

"No, sir," he said, in a choked voice, his eyes wide and wet.

"That's great. Thank you for your cooperation. Let's start with this: why did you try to run away just now?"

"I thought you were here to collect money."

"Are you late on the rent, Mr. Hattori?"

"No, sir."

"Who do you owe?"

"Chan Ho."

"I see. And why do you owe Mr. Ho money?"

"I just do, that's all." Some of his gumption had crept back with his breath.

"Mr. Hattori, you said you would answer my questions. I'll try one more time, and if you don't choose to be more forthcoming, you and I will take a little trip downtown. Under martial law, they can throw you in a jail, or a brig, or who knows where, and just forget about you. No writ of habeas corpus, no lawyer coming along to bail you out. Do we understand one another, Mr. Hattori?"

The last of the starch left him. "I owe him because I lost at fan-tan," he said, disappointed with himself.

I sighed, as if he were the prodigal son and I was searching for a way to forgive him and kill the fatted calf.

"I see. I'm disappointed in you, a college man and all. Surely you know that fan-tan is entirely based on luck and the deck is stacked against you. There is no skill involved whatsoever, which means the house will always prevail over the long term. Often the short term, for that matter. You should know better."

"Yes, sir."

"Now, see, we are getting somewhere. I may yet be able to keep you out of jail. Where were you the night of December 6, 1941—last Saturday night?"

"I know what you're really asking about. I was right here, at home."

"Not out playing fan-tan?"

"No, sir, I'm all out of credit."

"Was anyone with you while you were spending the entire night at home?"

"No, I was alone."

"What did you do, while you were home alone and not out playing fan-tan. And before you answer, consider that there were a lot of people out playing fan-tan and a good five percent of them are police informants of one kind or another."

"I was here, I swear."

"Doing what?"

"Nothing."

"Nothing?"

"I listened to the radio mostly. I may have had a beer or two. Ate some noodles, I think."

"After you listened to the radio and drank your beer and ate your noodles, did you walk down to School Street and shoot Daniel Nakajima in the head?"

"No, *sir.*"

"Are knife fights more your style?"

"Knife fights?" He seemed confused by the question. "No. I don't even own a knife, or a gun. Unless you count a kitchen knife or two."

"What about stolen property, do you have any of that? If I check your apartment, what will I find?"

He ground his jaw. "That was a bullshit charge. I bought a hot bike from a guy—I didn't know it was stolen."

"Then why did you plead guilty?"

"Just following my lawyer's advice. He said it would be easy for the prosecutor to convince the jury that I knew the bike was stolen because of what I paid for it."

"How much did you pay for it?"

"Two dollars and fifty cents."

I shook my head disapprovingly. "Your lawyer was right. You knew it was hot and no self-respecting juror could possibly think otherwise. Two dollars and fifty cents. Shame on you. You did know, right?"

"Not for sure."

"Why don't you show me your apartment? I might want to rent here myself, what with this nice lanai and all."

With a look of defeat, he stood up and fished a set of keys from his pocket. As we went in the back door, I made sure to account for any kitchen knives that might be lying around. The apartment could have benefited from a proper cleaning. There were dishes in the sink, dust mice on the linoleum floors, but nothing unusual for a single man in his mid-twenties, and nothing at all that looked like something anyone would bother to steal.

I gave him my card and extracted a promise that if he came to know anything about the Nakajima murder, he would be in touch.

"So, here is my advice to you, Mr. Hattori," I said, standing in his front doorway. "Give up the fan-tan. And don't let me hear you've been anywhere near Keiko Matsumo. Got it?"

Hattori said, "Yes, sir," then, as I turned to go, "Mr. Ross?"

"Yes?"

"You probably already know all about this, but not long before your partner, Mr. Heston, was killed, he won a whole bunch of money at Chan Ho's place. Some say it was the biggest pot ever."

#

CHAPTER 5

For the ten days since the attack, I had been living on lunches from the Times Square Grill on Hotel Street and dinners from the leftovers. I didn't have anything remotely edible left in the house on Paki, but I did have just enough time before curfew to swing through May's Market.

The paperboys out front were hawking the day's big story: Admiral Kimmel and General Short had been relieved of their commands. That seemed inevitable from the start, but I couldn't help thinking they drew the short straw. Everyone right up the chain of command bore responsibility for December 7, they were just the necessary scapegoats. On the other hand, it was impossible to argue with the fact that they had managed to get their commands shot all to hell.

In May's I looked for my friend Kennie, a young savant who was the world's best stock boy. Kennie was challenged in many ways, but he worked hard, he was always friendly, and he knew the aisle, shelf, and position of every last item in the place. Sometimes, if you didn't gently cut him off, he would tell you the current shelf position of whatever it was you were looking for, along with the one before that and the one before that.

When I found him, he was helping a professor from the University of Honolulu find the White Star Tuna.

"We're out of White Star, but it's normally on aisle three, left side, top shelf, halfway down. If you look just to the right of the Fish Harbor tuna packed in saltwater, you can't miss it. Except, we're out of that too. Next shipment is expected on December 22."

When the professor left, Kennie turned to me. "I love my

job. All day, really smart people ask me questions. And I'm the only one who knows the right answers."

"Remind me, Kennie, how many times have you won Employee of the Month?"

"Fifteen so far. But December will be over before you know it," he said with a predatory smile.

I asked Kennie where he was hiding the flashlight batteries and wished him a good day. There were a lot of bare places on the grocery shelves. There was no beef or chicken, btu I did get a decent piece of fish. In the cereal aisle, I had to settle for something called Shredded Ralston. The box, which bore an unsettling resemblance to the same company's checkered dog food packaging, encouraged me to "Get your whole wheat every day—the Shredded Ralston way."

I filled the saddlebags to overflowing, draped the gas mask bag over one shoulder, and wore one shopping bag like a backpack, at a bit of a cost to steering the bike. But I made it home unscathed, unloaded the groceries, and poured myself the very last drops of rye in my possession. If the liquor stores didn't re-open soon, the entire island might blow.

Now began the hardest part of life in Hawaii after the Japanese raid—the long dark night of the blackout. Not a glim of light could be seen from outside your residence. There had already been instances of wardens shooting out lights, with the occupants right there in the line of fire.

The blackout put you squarely on the horns of a dilemma. You could use the blackout curtains, but there went the normal air circulation that kept the house livable. With windows open and the trades blowing through, it was quite pleasant at night. Shut them, and it was a hot box.

Of course, you could open the curtains and windows, as long as no light whatsoever escaped. No cigarette glow. No illuminated radio dial. Not even a candle, lest that crafty old Yamamoto should spot it. Meanwhile, down the beach about ten miles, the lights on the docks at Pearl were blazing away. There was no way to fix all the ships that had been blown to hell unless the work never stopped. It was more than enough light to guide an enemy aircraft from twenty miles away.

I pulled the blackout curtains tightly shut, turned on the lights and began to look through the Heston murder file. It immediately felt still and close in the room.

The file was, as murder files go, a pretty thin one. It was unsettling to think that a life, or at least a death, could be summarized with such little expenditure of official paperwork. When Chief Michaels first came to Hawaii, from Oakland, in the mid-30s, he had put in place a whole raft of reforms. One of them was the creation of a standard format for the murder book, and that at least made things quicker and easier for me in the heat.

I liked to start with the photographs, in this case photostats, just to get re-oriented to the crime scene. They began with a wide, establishing shot of the area just east of the Makapuu Lookout, a favorite attraction of tourists by day and horny teenagers by night. It was on the Kalanianole Highway, near the extreme northeastern point of the island and it was, unsurprisingly, two teenagers intent on getting an early start on the evening who discovered the body.

After the wide shot came a medium shot of the area around the body and then closeups of the body and individual items of evidence, such as they were. There was a tight shot of a fraternity tattoo on Hes' right ankle: a small star and crescent design and the Greek letters Kappa Sigma.

Another series of closeups showed clumps of tobacco ash that had fallen onto the rocks, not far from the body. The ashes were consistent with the tobacco in two cigarillos Hes had in his jacket pocket, the kind he smoked incessantly.

There was the usual drawing of the scene, complete with measurements, a crime scene entry log (another of the chief's innovations) with just six names recorded, including Det. Tommy Ford, as the chief investigative officer. And a list of personal items found on the deceased: wallet with driver and P.I. licenses, a cigarette lighter, a grocery receipt, and twelve dollars in cash.

Aside from the photos, the autopsy report made up the bulk of the file, but only because it had to cover so many items, from the weight of major organs like the heart (312 grams), to stomach contents (roast pork and pineapple, easily one of the most common meals on the island).

The coroner found no defensive wounds, no other injuries except the one that was both the underlying and immediate cause of death—a gunshot to the head from both barrels of a shotgun.

I flipped through the rest of Coroner Hale's notes, trying not to drip sweat onto the paper. It was his job to determine not just cause of death, but the identity of the decedent, which he established on the basis of the tattoo, a positive identification by Marcia Heston, and most authoritatively, by fingerprints, taken before the body was even transported. The chain of custody notations indicated Tommy Ford had personally taken the fingerprint impressions from the body and matched them with the ones every member of the police department had in their personnel records.

When I turned over the last page, I could honestly say the Heston murder file had given me little more than a mild headache and a stifling house. But the Nakajima file was even less helpful. It comprised seven pages in total, most of them Hale's report that told me only one thing of note: the bullet that killed Daniel was a .22 caliber, recovered from the body. It was the weapon of choice for mob hitmen. I shut the Nakajima file and laid it atop the other. I turned off the lights, opened the curtains and stepped outside to cool off and clear my head.

It was a perfect Hawaiian evening, with a light breeze carrying the smell of hibiscus from the park. At least the Army hadn't managed to kill them yet. Back inside, I draped a piece of blackout cloth over the dial of the radio and turned it on. It warmed up slowly. I heard the fluid notes of a clarinet and the first notes of "Moonray," with Artie Shaw and his gang. The music spilled out of the big wooden cabinet and flowed across the floor. Helen Forrest's silky alto voice implored the moon to cast a spell on her lover, using all of its magic charms.

The song made me wonder what Nalani was doing now, not so far away, in her own little box of darkness. Did it smell like hot vacuum tubes, Old Golds, and fried fish? Did it sound like this? And why couldn't we be smelling it, and hearing it, and living it together?

I closed the curtains so I could see to clear the dishes and put the house in order. When I was done, I made the mistake of checking the mail. There was a single letter, from the National Service Department. The boldface headline at the top of the single page of paper hit me like a punch in the gut: NOTICE OF CALL-UP FOR SERVICE OVERSEAS WITH THE ARMED FORCES.

#

The next morning, I got into the office before Miss Kaimana. It was hot and dry again, more like summertime weather, so I opened the windows wider to catch the trades. From the sound of it, Honolulu traffic was picking up.

I put in a call to Dave Summers to see if he could help me figure out the best way to deal with a call-up notice. His assistant promised to give him the message.

Reading over the notice for the umpteenth time, I took heart in its vague, bureaucratic language: "You will be notified in due course by an authorized officer of the time and place for reporting." I was also more than willing to be encouraged by, "It is unnecessary for you to leave your employment until immediately prior to the date on which you may be required to report to a mobilization center."

It was all too easy to convince myself that I could put a lot of stock in that thin little "may." It worked every time, until I re-read the section that classified me as a Reservist of Class A of the First Division of the General Reserve. I tried to think of any way that might fail to mean I was in the first group. I had served Uncle Sam's Navy faithfully in the last one and seen things I never hoped to see again, but it wasn't that I was so much against going back into uniform, as I was determined to finish what I was working on first.

It didn't take much imagination to see the Pacific theater would be a blood bath for both sides before it was over, regardless of the outcome. It was bound to drag on for years— plenty of time for me to do my part. Right now, my best and highest use was solving a couple of murders that no one gave a damn about.

I noticed a scraping sound from the outer office and realized it had been going on for some time. I quietly got the gun from the safe, slowly opened the inner door, and looked out. There was a shadow behind the outer door. I eased over to the seldom used second door that opened onto the corridor and silently slid the coatrack out of the way. Slowly, I turned the deadbolt, then the knob. I flung it open and came out with the gun in my hand, pointed at the floor. A man in overalls with a razor blade in his hand jumped back, startled. I mumbled an apology, and he went back to scraping the door.

Miss Kaimana arrived promptly at eight, with her usual ebullience. Her energy, strangely enough, calmed my jangled nerves a bit.

"The sign will be done today, boss," she said in a tone that suggested she would paint it freehand herself.

"That's great," I said, "A new door could be just the break we need."

"There you go, pulling my leg again. Anyways, today is Wednesday, so I will call Mrs. Martin and schedule an appointment, yes?"

I said, "No. I don't have time for Mrs. Martin."

"We can't always count on having a murder case, boss," she said in a hectoring voice. "We may need Mrs. Martin to make payroll next month."

"We're fine on payroll."

She was unconvinced. "How about I call her, but ask her to come in on Friday?"

"Of *this* week?"

"Of course."

GUYMCCULLOUGH

"Okay. Make it in the afternoon," I said, trying to sound like I was still making the decisions.

She was pleased with her victory but tried to strike a magnanimous note. "Thank you, boss."

"I'm expecting a call at eight-thirty."

"Yes, boss."

#

Koga called right on time with Daniel's uncle already connected on the line. The three of us talked for one frustrating hour, with damned little to show for it afterward. For starters, it was a noisy line. The old man had trouble hearing Koga's slow, patient translations of my questions.

I learned Daniel spent very little time outside the house during his stay. Aside from his morning swims, and the trip to the doctor in Lihue, there was only one trip to get provisions, and that was to nearby Eleele. Daniel had been gone less than an hour and, when asked if he had seen any old friends, said no.

After we rang off, Koga called back immediately, mostly I think to commiserate with me over how little we had gleaned.

"Don't lose heart, Mac," he said, in a disheartened voice. We will work hard and be patient and one day, perhaps, luck will arrive."

"While we're waiting on luck, what do you say you ask Sato to tell me who killed my partner?"

"Sato-san is a man of his word. You will have your answer when the time comes."

#

I spent the next hour flipping slowly through the Heston file with the nagging feeling I was missing something. Miss Kaimana buzzed in on the intercom.

"You're all set to interview the ferry boat captain tomorrow morning at ten o'clock in the morning, boss." Then, in a questioning voice, she said, "There's an Osvaldo Ferrer here to see you, sir? He says he met you at his uncle's wedding luau."

"Okay, send him in."

A young man of about sixteen came confidently through the door and when we had shaken hands, rather firmly, he slipped languidly into the chair across from me. Picture, if you will, Errol Flynn in his mid-teens, right down to the dimple in the chin and the dark eyebrows. His dark hair was slicked back on one side and falling in waves onto his forehead on the other, but his sharp features and piercing brown eyes made a virtue of it.

"You must be Edward's nephew," I said brightly.

"I'm Osvaldo Ferrer," he said, with emphasis on the first name, "But my friends call me Oz, as in the Wizard of Oz. We met at the luau, remember?"

"Osvaldo, Oz, I have to be honest, your uncle's luau was quite a, quite an event. I'm not sure I can remember everything as well I might wish."

"Hey, it's okay, Mr. Ross. I understand," he said, pulling a pack of cigarettes from his pocket and shaking one out with a practiced gesture, "I was pretty tight myself that night. Hell of a party."

He lit the cigarette, took a deep drag, held it in his lungs, then looked up at the ceiling and slowly exhaled, in a move that would make Jimmy Cagney gape.

"Are you old enough to smoke those things?"

He glanced around as if to imply I must be talking to someone else. "I'm old enough to do a lot more than smoking, Mr. Ross. My parents know, if that's what you're asking."

"I'll take your word for it, Oz. So, how can I help you?"

"Oh, no, Mr. Ross. I'm here to help you. I knew when we met that night that we should be working together. You see, I have a network of guys—well there are a couple of girls, too. Mostly newsies, shoe-shine boys, messengers, a bunch of delivery guys for Western Union."

I vaguely recalled a conversation on the beach.

"You see, Mr. Ross, we find stuff nobody else can find. Kind of like the Baker Street Irregulars. We've memorized the silhouettes of every model of Japanese plane and ship in the fleet."

"Really?"

"Honest, Mr. Ross. Do you know how you can tell the difference in a Nachi-class and a Mogami-class cruiser, since they're almost exactly the same length?"

"I give up."

"I'll tell you how. The Mogami has five triple turrets, and the Nachi only twin turrets. We haven't been able to put stuff like that to much use yet, but we'll be ready when the time comes. We've made a killing on reward money. I keep a list. It's getting pretty damn long."

"That's very impressive, Oz, but I'm not sure how that helps me."

"Not that. But my crew hears things nobody else can hear, and sees things nobody else will ever see. At our age, it's sorta like we're invisible in a way, right? So, after the luau I got to thinking, maybe Mr. Ross could be our Sherlock Holmes."

"Well, I—"

"No, no. Don't sell yourself short. Uncle Edward says your pretty damn good."

"That's very kind of—"

"So, hear me out, Mr. Ross. I'm thinking we could come to some sort of arrangement. My guys go everywhere."

"What exactly did you have in mind?"

"When you need information or help finding something that's been lost, you pay us a dollar each a day and a twenty or so to the man who finds it."

Before I could reply, Oz thought of one more thing. "We'll need money for expenses, of course. Telegrams. Cab money, that sort of thing. But we will keep receipts. Proper accounting procedures are an important part of any job."

"I see."

"Don't worry. I'll manage all that for you," he said, blowing a smoke ring toward a window.

"So, you're to be my Wiggins, is that it?"

He smiled brightly. "I see you know your Holmes, Mr. Ross. We can do it just like with Wiggins. They report to me, and I report to you."

"Okay, Oz, but I will need to lay eyes on them at least to begin with. Just like Holmes, eh? And you have to understand that I can't guarantee work or afford to pay you anything at all when I'm not looking for something specific."

Oz had the good sense to realize that when you get to 'Yes,' it's time to quit selling. He popped out of the chair, snuffed out his cigarette in the ashtray on my desk, and extended his hand, all in a single motion.

"You've got yourself a deal, Mr. Ross."

This time I was prepared and avoided some of the bone popping force, by getting a bit of leverage on him.

"We're glad to be working with you, sir," he said, pumping my arm firmly. I had the distinct feeling I had just passed a job interview.

#

At 1000 the next morning, I called on the captain of the SS *Charon*, the inter-island ferry and cargo ship that brought Daniel home from Kauai the night he was killed. The boat (a ship technically, but us blue water sailors can be mighty stingy with that term) had been bought into the service. It was keeping its normal ferry schedule, but now it was dedicated to hauling military supplies and personnel to and from Kauai.

When I had hailed the officer of the deck, stated my business, and been invited aboard, I found the crew feverishly finishing the task of preparing to get underway for the return trip. The inbound cargo had been unloaded, and now, to shouted commands, the last of the Kauai-bound loads were being winched over the side and down into the hold.

With the help of the deck officer, I found Captain Jacobi in his tiny cabin just off the bridge. He was about my age, maybe a bit older, although it's sometimes hard to tell with a man who has made his living from the sea. When I questioned the captain about the night of December 6, he was unapologetically unhelpful.

"Mr. Ross, before the attack, our operation was quite simple. If you had a ticket, you got onboard. We didn't really care who you were or where you came from. Our service was an inter-territorial service—no visa, no passports, just a ticket."

"Was there a passenger list?"

"Not then. Now you have to have a chit from CINCPAC, and your name is entered in the ship's log. But that night, we were still a public ferry service."

I handed him Daniel's portrait photograph from the faculty section of his school's yearbook. "Any chance you remember this young man. He was shot and killed soon after he returned to Oahu on your ferry."

"I read about that in the papers, but there's really no chance I would have remembered or even seen him. Whenever we are entering or leaving port, or when I'm standing my watch, I'm always on the bridge. The rest of the time, to be honest, I'm usually in my cabin."

"Would you mind passing this photograph around to your crew at the next All Hands—in case anyone recalls anything that might be useful? A quarrel with another passenger, maybe."

"I'll do it in the morning. We will be at full complement then."

"What do you remember about that night?"

"I remember we were running way behind schedule all day, on account of a busted valve that took forever to fix. I checked the log and we got into Honolulu at 2105, over five hours late, so we were keen on turning it around quickly. That's where my focus was, as I am sure you can understand. Almost exactly two hours later, we had unloaded and reloaded, and we steamed out of the harbor for Lihue, arriving there a little after 0400 on Sunday."

"So, you would have left Lihue for Honolulu around 1600, is that right?"

"We can check the log, if you want me to be precise, but

very close to that time, yes sir."

"Let's say I was in Lihue, and I suddenly decided I wanted to be in Honolulu. How late could I have bought a ticket?"

"Well, right up until the moment we raised the gangplank."

"Suppose I bought a ticket and came to Honolulu, arriving at 2105, as you said. If I then decided that I wanted to return to Kauai, how would I know when to be back aboard the ship?"

"Well, we make a general announcement as we are pulling in. That night, we told returning passengers to be back aboard no later than 2300. I remember because I was determined for us to get headed back in order to be on time for the first Kauai to Oahu leg the next morning."

"And all I would have to do is to come to the Honolulu ticket office and buy a ticket before roughly that time?"

"Yes, sir. Unless you had bought a round-trip ticket on Kauai in the first place. Then you could come aboard at any time before we pulled up the gangplank."

"And to be certain, there's absolutely no record of who may have done so?"

"I wish I could say there was, Mr. Ross, but I'd be lying. The home office can probably tell you how many tickets were bought, and whether they were one-way or round-trip, but there would be no names recorded, as I said. Now, if you ask me about the eighth or any day thereafter, I can tell you exactly who was aboard any given leg."

I thanked the captain for his time and gave him my card. "If any of the crew recognize Daniel Nakajima from his photograph, please get in touch."

"I will. It's a shame what happened to that young man. Sounds like a dirty business"

"Thank you, captain. If, say next week, I needed to go to Kauai by boat rather than air, where would I start? There are a couple of potential witnesses I still need to interview on the island."

"Well, there I am going to have to disappoint you again,

I'm afraid. As a civilian, you're not likely to have much luck. Unless you happen to be buddies with CINCPAC, or someone on his staff, and even then, I suspect they are right busy at the moment."

#

Miss Kaimana looked up expectantly when I came through the door, which now read "Mac Ross, Confidential Investigations."

"You like, boss?"

"It's very nice, thank you."

Her look made it clear she was hoping for a greater demonstration of joy than I was prepared to give.

"He said it's some of his best work. But don't touch it for twenty-four hours, boss. Anyways, Tommy Ford called right after you left to tell you," she referred to the shorthand squiggles on her steno pad, "the man who called on Marcia Heston checks out."

"Great. Please call Marcia and tell her, with my compliments, that the detective who came to her house was on the up and up."

"With your compliments?"

"Sorry, that's an old habit. Tell her I said hello and I hope she is well, et cetera, et cetera."

She wrote on the pad. "Yes, boss. Et cetera, et cetera. Got it!"

"Thank you, Miss Kaimana. You're a great help to me, and I'm grateful."

"Ah, boss," she said, down inflecting the last word. "You're going to make me all teary eyed."

"Please don't. I'm headed to interview Mr. Nakajima."

She frowned deeply. "I'm so sorry, boss. That won't be fun. Please tell Mr. Nakajima that I am sorry for his loss."

"With your compliments?"

The smile returned.

"Yes, boss. With my compliments."

#

Koga met me at the Nakajima's modest home, in a lower-middle class section on the northern edge of Chinatown. He was there to be my interpreter, although Mr. Nakajima was said to have a little basic English. Interpreter was a job that conveniently, perhaps, allowed Koga to monitor my progress at close hand. As it happened, there wasn't any to monitor. Contrary to all logic and reason, I had pinned too much hope on the elder Mr. Nakajima as a source of leads. He had little to offer.

"My son got along with everyone, Mr. Ross," he said, genuinely perplexed as to why anyone would want to kill him. "He was a kind and gentle man, sir."

When I asked him about Daniel's statement that he had seen a ghost, he said, with help from Koga, it was a common belief at the plantation that the ghosts of the ancestors made an appearance from time to time.

"My brother has seen them. I can't say that I ever did."

"What about Daniel? Had he ever mentioned seeing ghosts before?"

Mr. Nakajima reverted to Japanese, looking at Koga with a misty pride in his eyes. Koga turned to me.

"Nakajima-san says to tell you that, past a certain age, Daniel didn't believe in ghosts. He says, Daniel was, after all, a teacher of science."

I bowed awkwardly, thanked Mr. Nakajima for his time and repeated my condolences.

And then, because I didn't have enough damn sense to keep my trap shut, I said, "Nakajima-san, I want you to know that I am going to find who killed your son. He deserves that."

He bowed deeply but didn't say a word. I got the feeling he wasn't betting on it.

#

CHAPTER 6

I spent the rest of the week getting nowhere fast. The only thing that kept me going was the thought of seeing Nalani at the end of the weekend. When the Sunday before Christmas finally arrived, it felt like the day itself.

I waited in the plush lobby of the Moana Hotel, double shaved and respectably attired. The roses in my hand looked artificial next to the red ginger flowers that seemed to be everywhere in the hotel. Despite our history, I felt like I was back in the first days of college, a frosh in a beanie cap, waiting self-consciously for my date to the first formal.

She came through the door wearing an elegant black dress, her hair in a chignon. It was a very different look from the earthiness of the fern bracelets, but she wore it equally well. I kissed her on the cheek.

"You look lovely," I said.

"Thank you, kind sir. You're not too shabby yourself."

We were shown into the dining room suspended over the empty beach, a beautiful view if you could block out the barbed wire. The waiter took our drink order, made much simpler by the fact that it was currently illegal to serve alcohol. Nalani asked if we could order lunch, since she had to be at work soon.

"Officially, we're working 10-hour days every day but Sunday, when we come in at two. But, most of us are there at least 12 hours."

I offered Nalani a cigarette, assuming she would decline since I'd never known her to smoke.

"Sure, I'll have one. I'm feeling festive, for a change." I lit hers and then one of my own. "How was your week, Mac. Are you still trying to find out who killed that nice young man?"

"Trying. Not making any progress. How about you? How do you like the new job?"

Nalani said, "It's been amazing to be in such a different world suddenly. I have to keep pinching myself."

"Well, that's good work if you can get it—pinching you."

She said, "Are you interested in applying for the job?"

"Very."

Nalani smiled and said, "But you haven't even asked how much it pays."

"Hard work is its own reward."

"Oh, my. I could use a man like you, then. I've been missing that Tingo Talango as of late."

"I'd be happy to help out. When is your next night off, sometime in June?"

"Hard to say. Right now, I'm having to stay late every night to reorganize the filing system. I inherited a first-class mess."

"I have a messy filing system, too, you know. What would be messier than a first-class mess?"

"I'd much rather work on yours than Uncle Sam's, even though he pays me. Of course, he doesn't pay all that well. It's nothing like what I made before, but that doesn't matter. The Bronx served its purpose, Mac, but I'm glad that's in the past now."

"Yes, it did serve its purpose. How is your mother?"

She put her hand atop mine. "She is good, thank you for asking. Her eyesight is fading fast, but she's very adaptable."

"That must run in the family, along with the good looks."

"I'll tell her you said so."

I had planned to mention the call-up order when the time was right, but about that time she put a second hand on mine. It didn't seem like the moment to say, "Oh, by the way, the Navy might send me away and I may never come back." Then lunch arrived, looking like it had been air mailed to us from the pre-war past, and we pried our hands apart.

"This looks yummy," she said, with a megawatt smile.

"Your ono looks nice."

"I've never been told that in my life. Thank you for noticing."

She laughed.

An hour glided by, a blissful interlude. She told me what she could about her job, which wasn't very much. I did gather that every military command on the island was desperately trying to manage the influx of troops and material being sent their way from the mainland. As lunch wound down, she noticed I hadn't eaten very much.

"Is everything okay with you, Mac? You seem pensive."

"I may have to consult a dictionary, but I'm pretty sure I'm fine. It's just that—I don't know. I want to take you places. See things. Go to a jazz club. Cook dinner together. All the things people do. Ah, I'm just babbling."

"Tell me about the jazz club. That sounds nice."

"Well, there's a great place in Chicago, called the Green Mill. Or, we could go to Old Havana, to a place called 'Abuela.' It's called that because it's the grandmother of all the jazz clubs there."

Nalani sighed. "Had we but world enough and time."

I must have looked surprised.

Her hand came back in search of mine. "I am an educated woman, you know. You may as well get used to it. And, for the record, I embrace the notion of seizing the day, and the night, and maybe the next morning, too." She laughed. "But there is world enough and time. Hell, two weeks ago, I was a working girl at The Bronx. Today, I have a security clearance. We just have to be patient, but enough about me, what's the hardest thing you are dealing with at the moment, dear man?"

"Well, I just got a call-up notice saying I'm in the first group to re-join the Navy."

She pulled her hand back, reflexively, then quickly returned it. I explained what it all meant along with my sneaking suspicion that someone was trying to get me out of Honolulu by giving me a one-way ticket to join the fleet.

"Mac, I can't explain why, but I believe it will all come right. Just keep moving forward. What you're doing is important. And surely your friends in the Navy can help."

"I hope so. But the Navy works in mysterious ways. It doesn't always make sense. It's all the more reason I want to know when I can see you again. And please don't tell me I have to wait another two weeks."

She wrinkled her brow, a look I hadn't seen before.

"I don't know, Mac. We're working Christmas Eve and even a half day on Christmas. And I'll need to spend some time with Mom when I'm not working. I can't leave her home alone on Christmas. What are you doing New Year's Eve?"

"I hope I'm cooking you dinner."

"I thought you said you imagined us cooking dinner together."

"Better still."

She brightened. "I bet we can make that happen. But it will only be our second date," she said, attempting to frown, but lapsing into a smile despite herself.

"It's okay," I winked. "There's world enough and time."

We took our time walking out through the ornate lobby. The familiar old hotel was somehow reassuring. At the entrance, the doorman whistled for a taxi. I opened the backseat door for her and tried to give her money for the fare, but she politely refused. As the taxi began to pull away, I motioned for the driver to stop. Nalani cranked down her window.

"You said you might give me your number."

"I was just waiting for you to ask." From her purse, she took a slip of paper and held it out the window. "Call me sometime."

#

My first call on Monday morning was to Dave Summers, to see what he could tell me about my chances for remaining in civilian life a little longer.

"Yeah, I've got something. But you're not going to believe

it. Let me find it on this desk of mine. Here we go. You were recommended for a return to duty by Commander Harry Somerville. Ever heard of him?"

"Doesn't ring any bells."

"Well, here's the crazy part. Commander Somerville was KIA on the Arizona. But his letter of recommendation wasn't mailed until a few days later."

"That is strange. Does that mean I can just ignore the call-up?"

Dave sighed. "No, it's not that simple. The call-up order is still valid until we can get someone to straighten this business out. I know a guy at J-1 who might be able to help. If you'd like, I'll check with him and get back to you."

"Yes, I would very much like it, Dave. Thanks."

"Yessiree. Be careful, huh? It looks to me like some son of a bitch wants you to be off sailing the bounding main. Must be a reason. Not somebody's husband I trust."

"Nothing like that, Dave, honest."

"Alright. I'll get back to you when I know something worth telling."

When I put the phone back in the cradle it rang. It was Peter Ochoa.

"Listen, Mac, I was on the beach just now and noticed someone looking around your shack. I slipped around and got a look at the registration on his car. The name is Moses Branco."

"Did he see you looking?"

"No, he was too busy checking to see if your windows were locked on the beach side."

"Good. Thanks, Peter. I'll check this guy out and let you know what I find."

I hung up and stared out my window. Someone somewhere wasn't happy with me. But I couldn't be sure whether it stemmed from the Heston, or the Nakajima case. Did this Moses Branco work for the Chairman? That seemed unlikely for a two-bit hood like him. There was a better chance he was mixed up somehow in the Nakajima murder. Maybe even the trigger man. When I turned back from the window, the walls felt a little closer.

I looked back at the telephone. For a week I had wanted to get some time with Jack Rogers, the FBI Special Agent in Charge for the Territory. But word was he'd spent the first ten days after the attack in his office, without going anywhere.

"Screw it," I said to myself, picking up the phone and dialing the familiar number: 4621. "All he can do is say 'no.'"

To my surprise, his secretary said, "One moment, please."

"Hello, Mac. How are you?"

"I'm good Jack. Well, not really, but thanks for asking. Listen, I know how busy you must be, so I'll get right to it. I'm working on the Nakajima murder, and I was wondering if I could get on your schedule for a half hour sometime this week or next."

There was a pause. "If you can come now, I can give you, say, fifteen minutes."

"I'll be right there."

I raced down the stairs—no time for OTIS—hopped on the bike and flew up the street and across the canal toward the FBI office on Dillingham, where Jack and a dozen or so of his special agents worked.

Since arriving in Honolulu, in '39, Jack Rogers had done more for race relations than anyone I knew of, burrowing into the *nisei* and Chinese communities and convincing their best leaders to join something he called the "Council on Inter-Racial Unity." Jack was convinced that fairness and *mahalo* were the keys to ensuring the safety and security of everyone in the islands. Some *haoles* thought he was crazy, but it was hard to argue with his results.

I was still a bit out of breath from running up the stairs when I was shown into his cluttered office. Tall stacks of paper were lined up across the desk and the credenza behind him.

"Hey, kid, good to see ya," Jack said in his southern accent, as I came through the door.

For some reason, he always called me, "kid," even though

he was just four years older than me. I had eventually concluded it was because he was the middle of ten children, and he had helped raise siblings not much younger than he.

"Thank you for taking the time. I know you don't have much of it to spare."

"Oh, I'd be fine if I didn't spend half my time trying to convince Washington not to lock up the entire Japanese-American population in the Territory, thus bringing the entire economy to a grinding halt."

"Really?"

"Yeah, Secretary Knox has it in his head that they are a threat to the operations at Pearl. I've told him over and over that the only threat to operations at Pearl would arise from locking them all up. And that, furthermore, there has not been a single credible instance of sabotage by anyone of Japanese ancestry, yet. Not one. I'm starting to sound like a broken record. And nobody in Washington seems to get the picture. How can I help *you*, Mac?"

"It's about the Nakajima case."

"Okay."

"Well, it slowly dawned on me that you have the best contacts among all of the various groups, especially the *nisei*. I was wondering if you wouldn't mind putting the word out, to see if we can stir up anything that might amount to a lead. At the moment I really don't have anything to go on."

"Sure. Happy to. There's something odd about that murder, Mac."

"I'll say. Daniel Nakajima is the least likely person to inspire murder in Hawaii, but for the fact that he did."

Rogers put his fingers in an inverted vee. "In my experience, Mac, the hardest murder cases to solve are the ones without any apparent motive."

"I thought maybe I was on to something with the ex-boyfriend of Daniel's fiancé, but it didn't hold up. So, I'm stuck, and although I know some *nisei*, my contacts can't begin to match yours."

He scribbled a note. "I'm happy to help, and here's something else I can do. When I'm not busy cajoling Washington, I'm wrangling with the Army and the Office of Naval Intelligence—your old outfit. I'll see if they know anything that might be helpful, though I wouldn't get my hopes up, if I were you."

"Thanks, Jack. I really appreciate it."

"Happy to help. I suppose you're no further along on finding out who killed your partner."

"You suppose correctly. I'm starting to think maybe I'm in the wrong business."

"Don't be ridiculous. You'll turn up something."

"At least I'm in good company. A detective from Frisco flew in to interrogate Marcia Heston. They apparently had two similar murders. It seems blowing someone's head off with a shotgun is all the rage these days."

Jack frowned. "Are you sure about that? They had two cases?"

"That's what he told Marcia, and I had Tommy Ford check him out."

"That doesn't sound right, Mac. First of all, if they had two cases like that, it should have been in the national crime summary I read every week from cover to cover. Not to mention the boys from Frisco always call us when they're in town, as a courtesy."

"Maybe, this guy wasn't the courteous type. He questioned Marcia the week before Pearl. He left her his card and his local number—the Royal Hawaiian. When I called, he had checked out, leaving the SPD as his forwarding address."

"Smells fishy to me. I would be shocked if there were two shotgun murders like that in the whole country. It's a very unusual method of committing homicide."

The hair on the back of my neck prickled. "We could find out for sure, if you don't mind cabling San Francisco."

"You draft the cable and leave it with my secretary. I'll see that it goes right out." He rose and extended his hand across the clutter.

"I'll do it right now. Thanks, Jack. Give my regards to Corrine." I left him sorting through his stacks.

#

I had ridden hell for leather to Jack's office. Now, I drove away at something barely above an idle. I didn't like the way my mind was turning, but I tried not to get ahead of myself. There was probably some simple explanation. In any event, it shouldn't take long to get an answer. I sped up and, at the corner of Beretania and Nuuana, there was Ah Nam Ho, back to directing traffic with his usual flair. Somehow it made me feel better. Maybe it was a sign that I *would* find the truth in time, like Wo Fat's fortune cookie prophesied.

At the office, Miss Kaimana was filing her nails as I came through the door. She looked at me reproachfully.

"Did you forget about Mrs. Martin," she asked, with parental disappointment in her voice.

I had. "Oh, damn it."

She smiled brightly and put down the file. "It's okay boss," she said," "She cancelled. She and Mr. Martin patched things up."

"Good."

"She offered to send you something for your trouble. Said it would have to come out of her pin money."

I stopped in my doorway. "If she calls back, please tell her to keep her pin money. She might need it for pins."

She chortled. "Should I tell her with your compliments?"

"Sure, why not."

I sat down just in time for the phone to ring. "I'll get it," I shouted.

It was Jack Rogers. "I thought I should call you myself. We got a quick answer for a change. Your man who questioned Marcia Heston did not come from SPD. They never heard of him."

I whistled.

"It gets better," he said, "or, I suppose I should say worse. The chief said it's been years since he's had a shotgun blast to the head."

"Well, I'll be damned."

"It sounds like Tommy Ford may have some explaining to do."

"I'll say."

"Well, I've always thought of him as a good cop, but unless you guys had some sort of misunderstanding—"

"No, I wish that was the case, Jack. Like you said, something's fishy."

"Be careful, Mac. You've got a permit to carry a weapon, I suggest you make good use of it."

"I will, Jack. Thanks again."

I sat staring at the phone, trying to think it through. I would have bet my house on Tommy Ford being a clean cop. But it was hard to come up with a plausible explanation. After looking at it from every angle, the only thing I could figure was Tommy had just been too damn busy to check it out, had concluded it must surely be legitimate, and had told me what I wanted to hear.

The only problem was that didn't sound like the man I knew either. And, if Tommy Ford had changed teams after all these years, it meant I couldn't trust that the Heston file he had given me was everything there was to see. I intended to find out.

#

I asked Miss Kaimana to stay as long as she could and still make it home before the blackout, just in case I needed her, then rode over to HPD headquarters. I parked up the block and walked down the alley to the back door, where my brilliant plan died a quick death. I thought, with any luck, my old key might still work in the back door. It didn't.

I considered going in the public entrance and somehow rigging the back door so I could get back in later. Maybe unscrewing the strike plate? But in the current atmosphere, anyone coming in the door would either have it fixed immediately or post a guard on it.

All out of ideas, I walked in the front door and tried to gauge whether I could just waltz into the records room like I'd been known to do. That's when I saw my buddy from San Jose State.

"Hey," I said, patting him on the back, "still working hard, I see."

He recognized me. "I'm getting the hang of it!"

"That's great. I've got a quick job for you."

"Okay."

I took a notebook from my pocket and wrote "Homicide: William Beauclerc Heston, III, October 23, 1941," tore the page out and handed it to him.

"Pop up to records and get me the full murder book for this case and meet me in the second-floor conference room, please."

"Sure thing."

#

When he came into the conference room, I was pretending to study my notes. I thanked him for the file.

"You're welcome. Back to the grind," he said, turning athletically on his heel and hurrying away.

I put the file under my shirt and walked stiffly out the back door, trying to be nonchalant. It felt thicker than the one Tommy had given me, but I told myself that was because I was smuggling it out in my pants. I forced myself to walk slowly to the bike, where I stuffed the file in the saddlebag next to my gas mask. There was only one place I could comfortably review it— my house. So, I headed there as fast as I could go through the pre-blackout traffic.

I gunned the bike with my throttle hand, the left, while waving apologies with my right as I edged around the congested traffic. Most motorcycles have the throttle on the right, but the Indian Motorcycle Manufacturing Company was determined to sell their bikes to police departments. So, on the Indian Four, they put the throttle on the left, leaving the gun hand free to fire.

Once home, I called Miss Kaimana to thank her and let her

know it was okay to leave and then proceeded to make myself a pretend drink, as in the good old days when there was alcohol in the house. I chipped some ice, put it in a glass, added water and a dash of bitters. I reached for the file, but something made me pick up the phone and call Tommy. He answered on the first ring.

"Hey, Mac, you caught me on my way out the door," he said. "It's my first night off since the seventh," honest excitement in his voice.

"That's great," I said, willing myself to sound calm and natural. "Say, I've been looking at the Heston file and just wanted to make sure of something. Is this the whole thing?"

"That's the whole kit and kaboodle," he said confidently.

"Okay, buddy, thanks. Enjoy your time off. You've earned it."

"Your damn right I have. Can't believe I'm this wound up about spending a quiet night at home."

I forced a laugh. "You must be getting old, like me. Have fun."

#

The two files were identical with one major difference: the original file included a confidential appendix. I read it through twice.

The upshot of it was that Hes Heston was a paid police informant and had been for quite some time. Tommy Ford was his contact officer and the two had met a little over an hour before Hes was shot at Makapuu point. Their meeting place was less than a mile and a half down the coast.

The notes of their meeting, signed by Tommy, said Hes was working on something big involving the major players in the opium trade and he expected to wrap it up soon. It was hard to imagine Hes as an informant. He had always had a certain contempt for people who sold information to the police, or even to us.

But, putting that aside, it looked like Tommy Ford had either killed Hes, or was covering up for someone who did.

Perhaps someone involved in the opium trade, as Sato was suspected of being. But if it was Sato, why would he hire me?

The second of my imaginary cocktails had no more of an effect than the first, except it knocked loose the memory of all the things Tommy had said or done of late. I played them back in my head, one by one.

On my birthday, at Wo Fat, he had very skillfully extracted a promise from me that I would keep him posted on anything I found out about the Heston case. *"You wouldn't leave me with my tits hanging out."*

He had also promoted his theory that Marcia had hired someone to kill Hes.

Looking back, Tommy had been keenly interested in whether I had agreed to take the Nakajima case. But none of that could hold a candle to the fact that he had managed to place someone inside my office, with easy access to my files and movements—even my finances.

Ford had been at the crime scene, one of only six entries in the log. But, far more damning, he had assured me the man who called on Marcia was on the up and up, and he had just told me the Heston file he copied for me was, *"the whole kit and kaboodle,"* when he knew damn well it wasn't.

On the other hand, he had cooperated whenever I asked for help—the cable I sent to the coroner, the night driving pass. I pulled the pass out of my wallet. It was time to use it. I retrieved my revolver from the gun safe and headed out the door, locking it behind me.

#

I don't remember anything about the trip from Waikiki to Tommy Ford's house in Pacific Heights, except thinking the place was only a quarter mile from where Daniel Nakajima was murdered. The house was twice the house Ford had lived in when we were partners, but that only made me compensate by questioning whether I was looking at everything through the wrong lens. People naturally trade up for a larger home when they can afford it.

Then I spied a ruby red '39 Packard convertible in the driveway, and all I could see was a gangster's car—right down to the wide, white sidewalls on the fat tires.

I knocked on the front door firmly, but politely. Old habits die hard.

"Hey, Tommy, open up. It's Mac."

Not a sound. I knocked again. No answer. I tried the knob and found it unlocked. The door opened slowly and silently.

From deeper in the house, I could hear Maxine Sullivan singing "My Blue Heaven."

I drew my gun and moved slowly from room to room, methodically and mechanically. I stopped short in the living room, where an oscillating pedestal fan made the curtain stir and settle, stir and settle, as it swept to and fro. I knew right away something was very wrong. The placid vocal notes of the song was strongly at odds with the atmosphere of the house.

I found Tommy Ford on his back in the kitchen, not more than a couple of steps from the backdoor, staring blankly at the ceiling, with a single, razor-clean cut from one side of his neck to the other. The pool of blood under him had just begun to congeal at the edges. No signs of forced entry or a struggle.

I went through his pockets, while Maxine sang about a smiling face, and a fireplace, and a cozy room. Tommy's back pocket still held his wallet. He had keys and a twenty in the right front. His body was still warm. I searched for a pulse, certain there wouldn't be one.

I picked up the phone, then put it back in the cradle. This was my one chance to look around the place. Nothing seemed out of order, or obviously missing. I re-checked both bedrooms and made quick work of the downstairs, which was one big room. Whoever had slit Tommy Ford's throat had not disturbed anything else, as far as I could see.

I looked quickly around his study, then checked the desk. Nothing seemed out of the ordinary until I got to the bottom drawer. It was completely empty. I went back to his bank book and rifled through it quickly. The only deposits were his paycheck, every other Friday.

I heard a floorboard and turned.

"Put the gun down and your hands up!"

It was Bing Williams and two uniformed officers, each pointing a gun at me. I sat mine down gently on the desk, slowly straightening back up, both hands where they could see them.

The music wound down: the brushes on the snare, a plaintive clarinet, a muted trumpet, and the final tinkling of the piano. It all played out, just as it was written, just as I had heard it dozens of times. Except this time, it sounded too much like my exit music in the great story of life. I stood there, like the fool I was, with my hands in the air. The only thing between me and Tommy and Daniel and Hes, waiting there across the River Styx, was four pounds of pressure on any one of three triggers.

The song ended, and "Stardust" began to play.

#

CHAPTER 7

It was a week before we could bury Tommy Ford. His only surviving relative—Aunt Maybelle—lived in Boston, which meant it took her the better part of four days just to get to San Francisco. Meanwhile, the Kona winds put in an appearance, and it rained off and on, the perfect accompaniment to my gloominess.

Every day I took a cab to the office and tried to keep my head down and look at everything with fresh eyes. Maybe it was the weather, but my mind kept returning to the fact that I had failed miserably. I was still uncertain how, or even if, Tommy was caught up in Hes' murder, but whether he was or whether he wasn't, I had underestimated the malignance I was up against.

I kept flipping back and forth between the conclusion that Tommy was corrupt or that I was simply ignorant of some essential fact proving his innocence. If Tommy was involved, he was killed because someone was afraid he might rat. If he wasn't involved, well, that was infinitely worse because it meant I had failed him, too. I wanted like hell to believe Tommy was the good cop I had known him to be as a partner, that he had nothing whatsoever to do with Hes stopping two blasts of buck shot with his face. Still, no matter how hard I tried, I couldn't come up with an innocent explanation for his behavior. I caught myself staring at the rain rattling ceaselessly on the windowpane, torturing myself with reproachful what-ifs.

What if I had figured out sooner that something wasn't right? What if I had just chosen to ask Tommy flat out about the appendix to the Heston murder file? And the best one of all: what if I had arrived at Tommy's house just a half hour earlier? He might still be alive, and Aunt Maybelle's greatest hardship would be weathering a New England winter in front of her fireplace, with a mug of tea and a Tabby on her lap.

Bing had let me go after taking my statement. He knew good and damned well I hadn't killed Tommy Ford, but I wasn't so certain. Normally, I'm not the kind of guy who indulges in self-recrimination. In fact, I'd always rather prided myself on accepting the inevitability of my own mistakes and moving on from them. But this was not a season of normalcy.

So, it only made sense that the winds would come to be backward too, with the leeward side of the island turned into the windward, and vice versa. It happened two or three times in the average year, but this time it was harder to take. Miss K said it had to be Keuakepo, the god of rain and fire. It didn't take much to convince me. I could feel his malevolent presence lurking somewhere just offshore, like a heavy static charge in the atmosphere.

Still, Kona winds are one thing, but combined with a blackout, it was sheer misery. Every night another cab dropped me off on Paki Avenue, like a prisoner on work release coming back to serve his time.

It was one of those nights, with the wind howling outside that I remembered the receipt. In all the excitement, I had simply forgotten about it. It was listed in the file Tommy Ford gave me, so I had no excuse.

The original murder book contained the receipt from May's Market found in Hes' back pocket. I looked it over thoroughly for the first time.

On the front, in perfect handwriting that reminded me of the anonymous letter, two items were listed: "Cigarettes, LS $.21" and "Peanut butter crackers $.09." The date was the day Hes was killed, October 24, 1941. The blanks for Address, Register Number, Account Number, and Clerk were all left blank. A red stamp marked the receipt PAID.

The thing that puzzled me most was why Hes would be buying cigarettes. The LS must surely mean Lucky Strikes. But in the more than twenty years I had known him, I had never once seen Hes Heston smoking a cigarette of any brand—even when he was out drinking and ran out of those noxious little cigars he favored.

Who was Hes buying cigarettes for on the day he copped it? Find the answer to that question and I might finally crack this thing.

I tried myself by court martial for not having given the receipt enough attention. My only defense was the revelations in the Confidential Addendum required my immediate attention. The voice in my head easily brushed that aside with the fact that, any way you sliced it, I'd managed to leave one of the precious few clues unexplored for almost a week. I found myself guilty as charged and, as punishment, spent the rest of a miserable evening brooding about it.

There was no taking solace in the bottom of a cocktail glass either. The bars and whiskey stores were still shuttered tight. In the end, the only thing that got me through it was the music—my records and the radio.

Since the day I had wondered into the Green Mill, jazz music, in all of its forms, had a hold on me. In the darkness of a Chicago night club, I heard a musical language for the first time that my heart seemed already to know.

I can't explain it, except to say it forced my mind to expand. I began to explore its roots in things like Cuban *contradanza* and ragtime, which I had paid scarce attention to until then. That led me, one by one, to the genius of Jelly Roll Morton, Louis Armstrong, King Oliver, Hoagy Carmichael, Bix Beiderbecke, and the incomparable Django Reinhardt. And, eventually, to more obscure musicians, like the Morales brothers and Julio Cueva, of Nalani's insightful birthday gift.

I enjoyed native Hawaiian music, too, but there just wasn't that much of the real thing on records. A lot of what got recorded had been westernized beyond recognition, but all of the local radio stations dedicated entire hours to Hawaiian tunes, played in-studio by local favorites, which meant the *haole* record producers didn't have a chance to screw it up.

Now, in the darkness, by the glow of a cigarette shielded from the uncurtained windows, the music kept my mind from consuming itself. It whisked me away—however briefly—to a happier place, where I could forget the war and the murders. I lost myself in the pulsating, syncopated, polyphonic wonder of it. Music and the prospect of getting to spend time with Nalani are the only things that kept me going.

#

First thing the next morning, I went to see Kennie at May's and showed him the receipt and Hes' photograph.

"Have you ever seen this man, Kennie?"

"No, sir."

"You're sure, not even once?"

"No, sir. I'd remember. He must shop at the Red & White or maybe Star Market, some folks do," he said with a mixture of sympathy and sadness.

I didn't want to point out that he must have shopped at May's at least once. Even Kennie's memory wasn't perfect. Or perhaps Hew was there in one of the few hours when the place was open for business, but Kennie wasn't working.

"I see there's a date, but why is the name and the rest of it left blank?"

Kenie pointed to the PAID stamp. "That's easy. The customer paid cash. You only need that information if it's a purchase to a house account. Cash and carry transactions don't need any of that. You wouldn't believe how much time that saves the cashier."

"So, there's no way to know, then, who wrote out the receipt? I was hoping the cashier might remember."

"I didn't say that Mr. Ross. I can tell that by the handwriting. The only cashier who writes like that is Orea Reeves."

"Is she working today?"

"No sir, Miss Reeves is off on Mondays and Saturdays and

after 2pm on Thursdays."

"Kennie, you've been very helpful. Thank you, sir." I extended my hand and he smiled and shook it.

"That's why I'm here, Mr. Ross. To answer everyone's questions." It wasn't lost on me that my job was to answer questions, too, but this kid was running circles around me.

The manager was polite but firm in explaining that he couldn't give Orea Reeves' phone number to just anyone who asked for it, so I borrowed his phonebook and looked it up myself.

#

Miss Reeves, a spinster with massive walnut furniture and enough elaborate lace doilies to choke a whale, could not have been more eager to help. She insisted on making coffee and when it was ready, we sat in the front room of her cottage. I started by complimenting her on her letter-perfect penmanship.

"Why, thank you, Mr. Ross. My dear late father insisted I learn shorthand, the Palmer Method and business English. He always used to say, 'It never hurts to have something to fall back on.'"

"I'm sorry, the Palmer Method?" The name range a distant bell.

She pointed to the receipt. "Yes, sir. That's what it's called. I have the diploma if you'd like to see it."

That's when I remembered where I had heard of the Palmer Method.

"Miss Reeves, I don't suppose you remember anything about the customer who bought these items."

"Oh, my." She was instantly crestfallen. "But Mr. Ross, I see so many. Why that's been nearly three months now."

"No, no, Miss Reeves. I had to ask. You've been very helpful. You've taught me about the Palmer Method."

She brightened, wanting to believe she had done well. "It is the best method by far, sir."

"I'm sure it is." I rose. "Thank you again, Miss Reeves. It's been a pleasure."

"But you haven't finished your coffee."

"Forgive me, Miss Reeves, but I really must run. I drank down a scalding mouthful to demonstrate my gratitude.

#

At the office, I glanced above Miss Kaimana's desk as I came through the door. There it was—the diploma, certifying her attainment of excellence in muscle movement writing, signed and sealed in San Francisco.

"Miss Kaimana, would you mind coming into my office. I need to test a theory."

She grabbed her steno pad and followed me.

"I would like you to write out for me—not in shorthand, but just legibly, the following words please."

When I had read the message in the anonymous letter, I asked her for the page. She looked puzzled but tore it out and handed it to me. It was indistinguishable from the original. Even the line breaks were the same.

"What's up, Boss?"

"Miss Kaimana, how many people have been trained to write like this?"

"The Palmer Method? Millions. It's been around forever, boss. But why did you want me to write that?" She pointed to the paper.

"Let me ask another way. How many in Honolulu?"

"I don't know, boss. There were twenty of us in the class at Honolulu School of Business, but it's taught at every busines academy that I know of. There are ads for it in all the papers."

I handed her the original letter. "Before you came to work for me, someone put this in my mailbox at home."

She looked it over, then apprehension dawning, back to me.

"But boss. Oh, boss. You don't think I would do such a thing do you? If I knew who killed your partner, I would just tell you."

I decided that if she had penned the letter, she was the greatest actress living, which seemed quite a stretch.

"So, if I had your twenty classmates in, they would write it just like this?"

She frowned. "Of course not, boss, there were only one or two of them as good as me. Anyways, I forgive you, boss. And if you don't mind me saying so, you need to go home and get some rest."

#

The morning of Tommy Ford's funeral dawned clear and bright, with a sharpness to the light and a hard edge to every shadow. The trade winds had, at last, come to their senses. It did nothing to heal me.

Aunt Maybelle, who turned out to be a fiery, take-charge sort of gal, insisted on a tasteful graveside service at the venerable Oahu Cemetery.

"The last thing Thomas would want," she said, "is someone using his funeral as an excuse to preach a sermon."

Just as the service was about to start, Nalani slipped into the aisle seat I had saved for her, looking like a prim yet earthy vision in her somber black dress and vibrant green *maile* funeral lei. Maybelle did acquiesce, with a firm-jawed dignity, in the matter of the twenty-one-gun salute, delivered by a police honor guard. The minister kept his remarks short and ecumenical. He knew a force of nature when he saw one.

Afterward, at the reception at Tommy's house, not altogether unlike the gathering for Daniel Nakajima, right down to the catered menu, I ran into Chief Michaels.

"I am very sorry for your loss, Mac," he said. "I know the two of you were close."

I nodded and said, "I'm sorry for yours, too, sir," uncertain as to whether his proper manners were because Nalani was on my arm.

Bing Williams was there but seemed intent on avoiding me. Aunt Maybelle was the only bright note, with as much salt and pepper in her personality as in her hair. She told me the story of how she had managed to reach Hawaii with such relative speed. While waiting for her train at South Station, she had called up her grade school friend, Frankie Knox, and talked her way onto a B-17 that was being sent to Oahu to beef up the aerial defenses. The same Frankie Knox known to the rest of us as the Secretary of the Navy, whom Jack Rogers spent so much time talking off the ledge about interning Japanese Americans in the territory.

I liked Maybelle immediately, and gave her my card, insisting she call me if there was anything I could do to be of help to her while she was in town settling Tommy's affairs. She promised she would, then went back to complimenting Nalani on her beauty, in the unbegrudging way of a woman who knows she was beautiful once in her own right and has made peace with beauty's fleeting nature.

"He was such a tender child, Mac. He went through a lot at a young age, but he never lost his tenderness," she said. "But then, I expect you know that."

I nodded and bowed, and we took our leave. As we turned to go, Maybelle grabbed me for a hug, with surprising strength and whispered in my ear, a bit loudly, "She's a keeper, Mac." That much I knew. The question in my mind was whether I was.

#

The next morning, I was in the offices of Col. Herbert Chatsworth, reading through the *Star-Bulletin* and waiting for the great man to see me. My buddy Dave seemed to think Chatsworth was my best chance to remain a civilian, at least long enough to complete my current assignments.

The newspapers were suddenly and stridently intent on making things seem as normal as possible, and they were not the only ones. A coalition of businesses went in together on a full-page ad that said it was "Business As Usual," which seemed absurdly delusional with all the shortages in supplies. An opinion piece downplayed the Japanese raid, saying it "wasn't what it was cracked up to be." Tell that to the several thousand dead Americans.

A photo on page two showed a beaming Arthur Okinaka, 14, handing over $300 he had raised to buy a Defense Bond. The Mutual Telephone Company advertisement warned Honolulu customers not to talk about the weather on the telephone. The art museum was reported to be burying a number of priceless paintings beneath the museum for the duration, which told me they must be hidden elsewhere.

Eventually, I was shown into the colonel's office, past the door that read "Deputy Director of Personnel (J-1), Hawaiian Garrison, T.H." Things started off well enough.

I laid it all out for the colonel, emphasizing that whoever had forged the letter recommending me had committed a criminal impersonation of a dead service man killed in action, and pointing out, calmly and rationally, how the entire basis for my call-up was completely bogus. Not to mention that I was engaged in work that had redeeming social value—potentially bringing as many as three murderers to justice, at a time when the Honolulu Police Department found itself overtaxed. I had done my part in the last war, eagerly and well by every possible measure (it's all there in my personnel file), and I was happy to do so again as soon as I had my affairs in order, which included solving three important cases that showed great promise (the latter being the only time I departed from the truth for the sake of emphasis).

Chatsworth didn't see it that way. On the wall behind him Franklin Delano Roosevelt also seemed to regard me with suspicion.

"I'm not sure why Dave sent you here, Mr. Ross," he said, looking over my call-up notice for a good half-minute. The clock on the wall was the only sound. Tick. Tick. Tick. I knew better than to fill the silence.

The Colonel's eyes completed the task of reading the notice. "First of all, this is not exactly my bailiwick," he said, looking back down at the notice and beginning, as his eyes betrayed, to read it again. I think he was hoping I would just give up and go away. I wasn't about to give him the satisfaction but, eventually, I would have to say something.

I cleared my throat. "Well, Dave seemed to think that since we know, for a verifiable fact, that the letter that started this ball rolling was falsified, you more than anyone on the island could put the kibosh on it."

I knew as soon as I had said it that I was just repeating the same argument. As if to confirm my idiocy, Chatsworth frowned deeply. Then looked at me as if he questioned my intelligence.

"I understand that Mr. Ross. Dave told me all about it. It's strange, I'll give you that," he said, as if he was actually giving me something. "But as sure as we sit here, you are designated NR1A —meaning you are classified as Class A in the First Division of the General Reserve. It's very straightforward, Mr. Ross. You're at the front of the line."

"But I'm forty-two years old, Colonel. Is that common?"

Chatsworth, who was the spitting image of an older William Faulkner, down to the moustache and the pipe, now looked disappointed. "No, no. It is not. But that's neither here nor there. The fact remains, without reference to whether it's *common* for someone of your age to be NR1A, that you *are* NR1A."

He tapped out his pipe and refilled it, from a bag of Captain Black at his elbow. When he was done, he lit it slowly, then began laying out a screen of smoke, like a destroyer going into battle. It seemed Col. Chatsworth and Captain Black were determined to open up a new front in the war.

Eventually, he said, "Mr. Ross, I'm afraid this war is a great inconvenience to all of us. But we can't go around exempting people who have been trained by our military establishment. Why, on that basis, we would soon find ourselves without an Army."

I was losing my patience. "But I wasn't in the Army, Colonel. I was in Naval Intelligence."

A series of looks came over his honest, Faulknerian face:

puzzlement, surprise, and—at last—an unmistakable gleam of triumph.

"Well, now wait just a damn minute, then. Did you say you were in the Navy?"

"Yes, sir. Several times." *Hush, Mac, you could still screw this up*, an inner voice scolded.

"Well, this notice," he said, holding it aloft in an entirely different way, as if now it had been transformed, through some obscure alchemy, into the hopelessly inflated currency of a banana republic, "has nothing to do with the Navy, sir."

"Then, I can ignore it?"

"Well, no, you can't ignore it. But, unless I am mistaken, Mr. Ross," he stood now, savoring the prospect of total victory over his sister branch and offered his hand. "Unless I am mistaken, I *can* put the kibosh on it." At this he put down the pipe and pumped my hands with both of his. "Call me at the end of the week. I believe you will be happy with what I have to report," he said, showing me to the door with a smug satisfaction.

#

The Colonel had put me in such a good mood, I decided to pay an unannounced visit on Nalani, whose office was just down the street from Chatsworth's weirdly futuristic bunker. Once there, I found the Officer of the Day, a wet-behind-the-ears lieutenant, who nonetheless had the good sense to know he was just that and who gladly offered up the administrative assistant to the Deputy Commander, for the purpose of visiting the mess hall (my second lie of the day).

More importantly, he was clever enough to wash his hands of all responsibility. "Sure, she gets a full thirty minutes. How she spends it is her own business." *This little Pontius Pilate will go far*, I thought.

For a moment, I couldn't tell whether Nalani was glad to see me, but once we left her coworkers, she visibly relaxed and regained her usual effervescence. I pointed at a hot dog cart on the sidewalk in front of the headquarters building, amid the whitewashed stones. "May I treat you to a hot dog, Mademoiselle?" I asked.

"Sure, big spender," she said, cocking the eyebrow in the way that made my knees weaken.

Only a fool failed to order a "special" at this particular stand. No one knew what was in it, but it tasted so good that ignorance was sweet bliss. When I told Nalani that my meeting, while apparently a good one, still left me in need of a drink, the Greek owner of the stand, whom everyone called Papa Papadopoulos, listened discreetly. After he served up our dogs, he offered me a large flask from his apron pocket.

I took a modest pull. It tasted like the grappa I had sampled liberally on an Italian ship we had boarded and commandeered in the last war. If anything, it had a greater kick.

"Good," I said, willing my throat not to close up. "Strong, too," I croaked. "It tastes like grappa."

Papa smiled and nodded knowingly, slipping the flask back into a gusseted pocket "It's a good-a for the pipes," he said. Then, after a pause, in which he took the flask back from the pocket and tippled, "We Greeks make the best grappa. Except we call it *tsipouro*."

I ordered a bag of hot cashews, to help with the lasting aftertaste of skins and stems that were the basis for grappa and this concoction that looked like water and tasted like fire. When we had our specials and cashews (added without charge "for the beautiful lady"), we wandered off to picnic tables that had been set up to accommodate all of the new arrivals flooding the canteens and mess halls. The wood was still green and sappy in spots in the sunlight.

"I'm sorry to drop in on you, but I really was in the neighborhood," I said.

"I'm glad you did. It's always good to see you, Mac," she said, with a smile that made my heart feel quivery.

"I've missed you," I said.

"I've missed seeing you, too. I guess this is our second

date, huh?"

"I guess it is. Sorry, there's not much to it."

"I'm not. I never thought I'd have such a wonderful lunch break," she said, with a smile and an eyebrow. Then, impishly, "Next time will be our third date. You know what they say about that."

"That it's better than the second? I can't imagine how. Are we still on for New Year's Eve?"

"Turns out, I don't have any plans."

"Then let's make dinner together. I have a night pass, so I can take you home."

"Who knows. Maybe you won't need it."

#

Oz was waiting on me at my office, as if he had read my mind on the ride back from lunch. He was chatting along charmingly with Miss K when I came through the door, one leg flung over the arm rest of his chair. He straightened up as I tossed my hat on the coatrack and missed, again. He scooped it up and put it atop the rack.

"How goes it, Mr. R?"

"Not bad, not bad, Oz. I think I have a little job for you. Come into my office and I'll tell you about it."

I decided I had let the Moses Branco angle go long enough. Branco didn't show up on any national criminal database, so I had discounted the whole thing. With Tommy gone and Bing no longer in what you might call the friend's column, I couldn't just pick up the phone and get an answer, and I hadn't made it enough of a priority to take a cab through the rain to HPD and finagle Branco's rap sheet. Then it dawned on me that doing a work-up on Branco was the perfect way for Oz to earn his stripes. He could provide the shoe leather and stay well out of harm's way.

When I gave Oz the background on Peter Ochoa's call, he whistled.

"Give me a couple of days, Mr. Ross. I'll tell you his shoe

size."

"Just don't get too close to him, okay?"

"I won't"

"Promise me, Oz."

"I promise, I swear."

When he had gone, Miss Kaimana tapped on my door and entered without waiting. "He's as cute as he can be," she said, inclining her head in the direction of Oz's departure.

"He's sixteen."

She shot me a withering look. "I didn't mean that way, boss. Anyways, someone named Kathleen Berry left a message. Said to please call her."

"I don't know a Kathleen Berry," I said to her back, then realized the number was the one for The Bronx. It had to be Vassar's real name.

She answered on the first ring.

"Have you changed jobs?" I asked. "You're the receptionist now? Or did you go straight to Madam?"

"No, I'm still plying my trade. Well, I will be next week, when we reopen, if I haven't forgotten how to do it."

"As far as I can tell, it's like riding a bicycle."

"I wouldn't know anything about bicycles, Mac. Haven't you heard? I have a new car. I need to take you for a ride, but that's not why I called."

"I've been taken for a ride before. At this point, I think I'm being taken for a ride about being taken for a ride, if you know what I mean."

"Just say when, Mac. In the meantime, I wanted you to know our revolutionary forces have come under attack."

She described a party she had thrown in Waikiki that went into the night. When the neighbors complained, the HPD got involved.

"They were going to take me to jail, Mac, can you believe it? Nobody else at the party, just me. If the MPs hadn't shown up, they would have."

"So, Michaels is determined to enforce the Ten

Commandments, huh? As I recall, Waikiki is off limits."

"Along with any place else you'd care to be seen. It sure looks like that asshole is sticking to his guns. And that he wants to make an example out of yours truly. Any thoughts?"

"Just one. You need a lawyer on retainer—someone with the clout to get you out quickly if they come up with a way to throw you in the clinker. Once you are in there, you are at their mercy. And with martial law, even an attorney may have trouble springing you."

"Well, that's not very comforting, Mac."

"If you're looking for comfort, you should call a priest. I'm just giving you the facts of life. But don't worry. Let me make a phone call. Someone will be in touch."

"You're a true friend to the revolution, Mac, and I'll never forget you for it. If you weren't prowling around Nalani, I'd be tempted to offer you a free and open exchange of goods and services."

"I'm not prowling. But if I was not bespoke, or hoping to be at least, I'd be sorely tempted to take you up on it."

"You'd be sore, that's for sure," she said, with a chortle. "The revolution thanks you."

"You can thank me by staying out of trouble at least until we get you a lawyer. Obey all traffic laws. Don't spit on the sidewalk. Comport yourself with poise and decorum at all times."

She sighed, resigned to her own destiny. "I make no hollow promises."

"At least you are honest about it."

"It *is* the best policy, Mac."

#

I called Warren Sears, the best criminal lawyer in the Territory, explained the situation with the Ten Commandments, with which he was thoroughly familiar, and asked him to get in touch with Vassar, giving him enough background to make certain he knew the power of the intellect he was dealing with, and urging him to go easy on the fee.

"No problem, Mac. I get the picture," he said, "It will be worth it to me to take a poke at Michaels."

As I put the phone back in the cradle, Miss K hurried into my office. "Marcia Heston on line one, boss. She sounds upset."

I scooped up the phone and fumbled for a cigarette. "Marcia, are you okay?"

"I'm okay, but the house is a wreck. I just got home from the hospital. Someone's broken in and ransacked the place."

I dropped the cigarette in the ashtray. "I'll be right there. Get in your car and pull out into the street. Keep a sharp eye out all around you. If you see anyone but me or a cop, drive away like a bat out of hell and go to the precinct. Will you?"

"Yes, yes, Mac."

"Go now please."

She whispered, "You don't think they are still in here, do you?"

"Go!"

#

Marcia's house was a wreck alright. Every piece of art had been ripped off the wall. Every book pulled off the bookshelves. Little else seemed disturbed. In the hallway that ran almost the full length of the downstairs, every square inch of wall space had once been filled—from floor to ceiling—with family photographs and candids dating back to Hes' college days. Now, the walls were completely bare, the framed pieces piled high on the floor, some with broken glass. There must have been seventy or more photographs on the floor.

"This looks like someone was in a hurry to find a safe. Is there one?"

Marcia looked at me meaningfully. "Come with me."

In the master bedroom, a large piece of original art, a sort of expressionist landscape of the Nuuana Pali Lookout lay face forward, cocked at an angle against the wall. Where it had once hung, there was a safe with the door askew.

"What was in it?"

"Nothing as far as I know. I never had the combination. It was in the house when we bought it. I never even saw Hes use it. We had a safety deposit box at Bishop Bank for that sort of thing."

I looked closely at the safe. "Whoever cracked it knew what they were doing. Have you called the police?"

"I called *you*."

"Okay, we may as well get that over with."

Marcia took a deep breath. "Will you call them?"

"I will, but you'll need to speak with whomever they send out. He'll have questions I can't answer."

She sighed. "Okay, but first let me put on a pot of coffee."

When the detective arrived, looking all of twelve years old, he was nice and deferential, not surprising given the address and the complainant.

"Do you know what is missing," he asked.

"It's hard to say until I can get someone to clean this mess up. Nothing I'm aware of."

He left his number and promised to check back before the week was out. "I can tell you that we will definitely step-up patrols in the area," he said, unconvincingly, in a voice that reminded me of the innumerable times I had made the same assurance, knowing it might not be true, but hoping it offered some peace of mind to a homeowner who felt violated.

When he left, we took our coffee onto the lanai, the only area of the house left untouched.

"Hang on a sec," she said, going back into the house, returning with a bottle of Jameson's. "It's the last bottle left in the house, but this seems like the right time to crack it open." She poured a generous amount into my coffee cup, then one of equal proportions into her own.

I asked, "Any idea what they could have been after?"

"I can't imagine. All of my diamonds are at the bank. I've had no reason to wear them since Hes died. He has some guns in the gun safe, downstairs, but you saw it—they didn't touch that."

"These guys won't be back. That's not how they operate. But do you have someone who can stay with you for a few days? Just so you'll feel safer."

She considered. "We used to get the gardener to spend the night in the guest house when Hes travelled to the mainland or Australia. It's wired into the phone system. But I'll be fine, Mac. As my mother used to say, 'I'm not made of cotton candy.'"

"That much I do know," I said, "But I'll feel better if you ask him to stay for a week or so. Will you do that for me? Having your most private places invaded works on your head, I don't care how strong you are."

"I'll call him. And I'll ask the neighbors to keep an eye out."

"Thank you. How's your volunteer job at the hospital going?"

Marcia's eyes lit up. "It's wonderful to have something to get out of bed for Mac. How about some more coffee? There's plenty of whiskey left."

"Don't tempt me. It's the only whiskey I've had in weeks. I'd better get going before the blackout."

"Oh, Jesus, how I hate the blackout. With or without whiskey. Mac, have you had any luck finding out who killed that nice Nakajima lad?"

"Not yet."

"He taught our Evelyn science, you know. She really liked him. I haven't had the heart to write her and give her the bad news."

The doorbell rang, or rather, it chimed. In a neighborhood like Marcia's, ringing was frowned upon.

"That must be the locksmith," I said. "He's going to fix the back door, and change the front door locks, too."

"Thanks, Mac. I'll sleep better. And so will the gardener. He's not exactly Charles Atlas."

"My service always knows where to reach me. Do not hesitate. I can be here in no time."

I cranked the bike and rode slowly toward Waikiki, my

mind turning on why anyone would want to break into Marcia Heston's house. It was a prosperous looking place, to be sure, with one of the first private swimming pools on the island, but the little voice in the back of my head told me it wasn't as simple as that.

Marcia's empty safe brought to mind Tommy Ford's empty drawer, which made me wonder—through some bizarre form of detective logic—if maybe they were somehow connected. All around me, Oahu had returned to its peaceful self. But inside my head, the Kona winds were still raging.

#

CHAPTER 8

The week had begun with a funeral on Sunday. Now, it was Tuesday and, as the Fates would have it, the time had come for a party—George Koga's *bonenkai*.

A *bonenkai*, as pretty nearly everyone on the island knew, was the most liquid of parties on the Japanese calendar. By design, it's a party at which one gets thoroughly sloshed, so as to forget the old year as a step toward clearing the decks for the new one to come. It was going to take a lot of *shochu* and *yuzushu,* sake and beer, to forget 1941.

Koga's house was only a two-minute ride from my place on Paki, just around a corner and up the northwest slope of Diamond Head. But, as with our offices, the social territory traversed was vast.

My neighbors were solidly middle class, but Koga's home was a literal stone's throw from La Pietra, Walter Dillingham's estate, built on ground once part of the temple where King Kamehameha had sacrificed the chief of Oahu and united the Hawaiian Islands for the first time. By ending the *kapu* system in favor of Christianity, in 1856, the *haole* elites managed to get their hands on several royal sites, including the temple where King K once put the skull of his late rival on display. By the turn of the century, the wealthiest *haole*s began building homes in the area. La Pietra, just up the slope a few feet from Koga's place, was the grandest among them. On the other hand, Koga had nothing to be ashamed of.

The house was set on a promontory in the center of an immense grove of doum palms that began within mere feet of the house on every side and continued outward away from it in ranks, until the most distant trunks appeared to merge. The trees nearest the house arched up and away from the elegant wooden structure. Their branched trunks, uncommon in palms, gave the setting an otherworldly feel. Near the floor to ceiling windows, gaps had been left in the trees, allowing light in and views out.

At the entrance, a pair of doors opened onto a *genkan* —a traditional Japanese greeting space. Inside, neatly arranged shoes lined the wall to the right, and rows of felt slippers the left-hand side of the room. When I placed my brogans at the end of the line, they stood out from their more sober neighbors. I crossed the room self-consciously, in my sock feet, and put on the pair of slippers exactly opposite my shoes.

The slippers took a bit of getting used to. I shuffled awkwardly through a door and into a large open room, where Koga was receiving guests. He gave me a quick bow and a firm handshake.

"Welcome, Ross-san. It's good to see you. Are you ready to forget the year?"

"I would gladly forget almost all of it."

"Well, that means something good must have happened in this *annus horribilis*," he said with his measured smile. "Very few of us can assert such a claim."

"I am a fortunate man, Mr. Koga," I said.

He bowed again. "Well, for those portions of the year you do wish to erase from your memory, we have laid in a supply of helpful libations. For your convenience, there is a bar in the dining room," he gestured across to a sunken room on the left, "and another on the lanai," pointing past a sliding *shoji* screen that was left open to the trade winds.

I chose the bar in the dining room, not because the weather wasn't fine—midday clouds had vanished leaving the afternoon sunny and bright—but because it was all the better for gawking at Koga's tastefully decorated home. A liveried bartender poured me a Haig and Haig scotch on the rocks. Just seeing the dark-honey color in the glass was enough to intoxicate me.

Koga's home embodied a balance between competing contradictions. Eastern and Western. Modern, but with timeless elements. It was spare, yet somehow had a lushness about it. The furniture was not low to the ground in the Japanese style. The lamps were western spindles

Milling about in all this splendor was a colonial mix of well-scrubbed guests, dressed in various degrees of finery, from white tie to full Scottish regalia. *Haole*s in tropical business suits and dress uniforms mingled effortlessly with the wealthiest of the Chinese and Japanese merchant classes, chatting amiably and drinking heartily, like a good *Bodenkai* guest should.

Around the walls were elegantly framed Japanese woodcuts, including a few that were Hiroshige and Masanabu, or very fine imitations. On another wall, a single Chinese ideogram, rendered three feet tall on parchment paper in exquisite calligraphy. It was one I happened to know— "Hope." Since Hawaii was one of the few places filled with westerners who could discern the differences between Asian cultures, I couldn't help wondering if Koga's display of that particular Chinese character wasn't perhaps a coded commentary on Japan's invasion of China in '37.

Throughout the downstairs rooms, the palette was the brown of bamboo and maple and the green of more than a half dozen bonsai trees of various sizes, from tiny to remarkably large, scattered throughout the space in a seemingly random fashion that nonetheless betrayed a careful eye.

Above us, in the center of the roof, was a large skylight and, above that, some nimble fellow had cut a swath across the canopy, allowing bright, diffuse light to fill the room. The effect of it all was to bring the outdoor landscape—visible through the oversized window frames—indoors, and to make the walls fade away.

The sunken dining room was a slightly darker, more intimate space, with tone-on-tone inlaid mahogany and an elaborate tapestry that must have been as costly as my house.

You couldn't tell there was a war on by looking at Koga's massive console table, every space covered with food: a simmering Japanese hot pot, heaps of edamame, and trays of *sashimi* and *yakatori.*

Koga appeared in the doorway, a raised glass in hand to get our attention, then stepped back into the center of the main room. He was far too mannerly to go around clanking cutlery on a glass, like us *haoles.* Guests from the lanai crowded into the room.

"Ladies and gentlemen, thank you for coming to our little *bonenkai*, a tradition begun long ago by the samurai lords. On this day, we have but one mission: to forget the old year, in order to be prepared to greet the new one in two days' time. In their wisdom, our ancestors arranged it thusly, so that we always have a full day to nurse our hangovers."

The guests laughed in good-natured unison. Koga paused, with the timing of a stage performer, then raised the glass again.

"So, dear friends, let us drink and forget. And we'd better get cracking if we are to beat the curfew. Here's to remembering our ancestors, even while forgetting 1941. *Kanpai!*"

"*Kanpai,*" we all said, and drank up. Everyone seemed highly committed to the mission.

#

Over the course of the next hour, the hum of all that forgetting grew noticeably louder, as inhibitions relaxed, and voices grew bolder. For my part, I soon realized that in less than a month I had grown out of practice as a drinker. I decided I had better go easy on the sauce, so as to be sure to remember to forget.

Outside on the lanai, an older, professorial gentleman with glasses and a well-groomed goatee was reciting poetry to a group of rapt listeners, some seated in satiny teak furniture, others standing. I slipped into the back of the clutch.

"This one," he said, with a softness of voice that made everyone lean forward, "is also by Basho, perhaps the greatest of them all." He paused, then began in a stronger, hieratical voice, firstly in Japanese, then in English.

Pausing between clouds
The moon rests
In the eyes of its beholders

Then, with hardly a pause, "This next one is by Issa, and it speaks to our current circumstances."

In our world
We walk suspended over hell
Admiring flowers

I slipped away amid murmurs of assent and a heavy sigh from an *haole* woman in a silk print dress with a florid face.

"Ah, there you are," Koga said. "I wonder if we might have a word while there's still time."

#

Koga led me up a spiral staircase to the second floor, where we made our way down a long hallway, past well-appointed rooms to Koga's capacious, booklined study. A huge globe dominated one corner. A massive desk with a sofa and two chairs in front of it. He offered me a seat, freshened my drink, and proffered cigars from a box of Partagas Coronas.

I took one and brought him up to date on developments in the Nakajima case, mostly a laundry list of dead ends. I explained that my man in Frisco was working on the wire transfer Hes had made right before he died. Koga held his drink up to the soft light from his desk lamp, rolled the ice around gently in the cut glass, then took a contemplative sip.

"Any leads on who killed Tommy Ford?"

"Not really. None of the neighbors saw or heard a thing." I didn't go into my own misgivings about Tommy. No sense slandering the dead to no practical effect. I took a drink, and decided to ask Koga a question I had been wanting to ask for some time.

"How much do you know about the opium trade in the territory, Mr. Koga?"

Koga looked sideways at me, then made an elaborate show of lighting his cigar. He made a neat cut of just the tip, with a large amber guillotine cutter. He took a long, wooden match from a group of them in a match holder on the table between us, creased it with his thumb and waited while it flared and burned off all the sulphur on the head. He held the Partagas at an angle, between thumb and index finger and toasted it, holding the match an inch or so from the foot, so that it was just out of reach of the flame, gently rotating the corona to heat it evenly.

Only then did Koga put the very tip of the cigar in his mouth, almost primly. The long match was burned halfway now. He took short puffs, like a train leaving the station with increasing speed, drawing the flame into the tip until it was fully and evenly lit. Then, he took a proper draw, rolling it around in his mouth like a fine wine.

"Very little, really," he said at last. "I doubt I know as much as you. I've heard rumors about who the major players are, but then again, Sato-san is so rumored, and I know that is not true. I do know that among some of our Chinese friends, including a few who are here today, a discrete pipe every now and again is considered a part of the good life—nothing more."

"An illegal one, however," I said, then immediately wished I hadn't.

Koga gave me another meaningful look. "Careful, Mac," he said, swirling the glass again and holding it up as if to inspect it. "You might not want anyone to inquire too closely into the legality of your own recreational pursuits."

I looked at my glass. He had a point.

"I didn't mean to imply any judgement. Merely to state the fact. Strictly between us, Hes Heston was acting as a police informant when he was killed. He told his police handler he expected to have the goods on someone involved in the opium business by the next day. Two hours later, he was lying dead at

Makapuu Point."

"You know for a fact he said that?"

I nodded. "Care to guess who his handler was?"

Koga tilted back in his chair, taking a draw and blowing the smoke toward the window. "I'm going to say Tommy Ford."

I nodded again.

Koga whistled and, for an instant, I saw the young boy he once must have been, before he learned to decorate a house or properly light a three-dollar cigar.

"Damnation, Mac," Koga said. "It looks like the time has come for me to get better educated on the poppy."

#

CHAPTER 9

OTIS took its usual time inching its way up to my floor. As it clanged and jerked, I realized, in a kind of minor epiphany, that its slowness gave me time to clear my head before starting the day. I developed a secret hope that the superintendent would never get around to having it fixed. Knowing our super, the odds had to be heavily in my favor. It was a good two minutes later before I exited the car. I heard Miss Kaimani typing at a furious rate, the keys like a machine gun—Rat-a-tat-tat.

Inside, I tossed my hat onto the top of the coatrack.

"Good moring, boss," Miss K said brightly.

I said, "You're in mighty early."

"Oz asked me to type his report, so it would be ready when you got here, but you're early. Just let me finish the last page.," she said, reproachfully.

"Oz's report?"

"Yes, boss," she said, then, in an exaggerated tone that ascended the musical scale with each word, "You're not going to believe it!"

She looked at a neatly hand-printed sheet on her copy stand, fired off another round of letters, pulled the typing paper out from around the platen, and placed the sheet on top of the others, face down on her desk. She took up all of the pages, gave them a firm rap on top and bottom to line up the pages and added a paper clip. Then, ceremoniously, she walked it into my office and placed it on my desk with a flourish.

"Wow, this must be good."

"Like I said. You are not going to believe it."

I lit an Old Gold and picked up the report. It ran to three pages. The heading read: "Overnight Surveillance and Investigation of MOSES 'MONEY' BRANCO."

SUMMARY FINDINGS

A team of investigators applied surveillance and investigative techniques to SUBJECT MOSES BRANCO, alias MONEY BRANCO, alias MARTY BROWN.

Commencing at 1700 hours on Tuesday, December 30, 1941 and continuing through 0600 on December 31, SUBJECT was observed at his home at 822-D Lopez Lane, in the Palama neighborhood of Honolulu, where he pays $49 per month to rent a one-bedroom/one-bath apartment.

Until the early morning hours, SUBJECT was seen drinking beer and listening to the radio. From time to time he spoke on the telephone. During two conversations, he referred to a racing form and a tout sheet. After consuming at least six beers, SUBJECT began acting abusively toward his common law wife, GLADYS FOSTER. BRANCO's phone rang around 0130, going unanswered.

SUBJECT never left the residence, nor did he receive any visitors during the overnight hours. However, at or around 0324, an UNKNOWN SUBJECT was heard opening the door to BRANCO's vehicle (1934 Packard, Black, Territorial license plate #32-281, expired November 1941). The UNKNOWN SUBJECT appears to have placed a sheet of notepaper on the driver's side floorboard. An operative copied the message and placed and oriented the sheet exactly as he found it. The message read as follows:

Hey, Money, I followed our little friend to a fancy party halfway up Diamond Head. Afterwards he went straight home. Lights out by 10:30. I kept checking

until after midnight, like you told me, but he never did leave. I'm telling you, buddy, get me $500 and I will take care of this problem for good.
(signed) T

BRANCO is a habitual criminal with an extensive history of incarceration in the Territory of Hawaii (see attached photostat). He has no discernible means of support and is not shown as having filed a Territorial personal income tax return for tax year 1940. There has been insufficient time and opportunity to interview neighbors without drawing attention to our surveillance.

PHYSICAL DESCRIPTION: MOSES BRANCO, alias MONEY BRANCO, alias MARTY BROWN.
BRANCO is 5', 10-11" and weighs 185 to 190lbs. He has sparse, black hair and a tattoo of an anchor on his right forearm, crossed cannons on his left forearm, and a design featuring a dagger through a swallow on his upper left arm. These distinguishing marks most commonly signify a veteran of the Navy, service as a Gunner's Mate, and the loss of a close comrade at sea, respectively. An unofficial review of naval archives is underway.

RECOMMENDATIONS: The investigative team recommends surveillance be continued on subject BRANCO, to include covert removal and examination of his household refuse, at such time as it is next placed at the curb.

Respectfully submitted to Mac Ross, Confidential Investigations, Inc., Honolulu, U.S. Territory of Hawaii.

Osvaldo Ferrer
December 31, 1941
  Enclosure: Expense Receipts

I was still looking at the report and shaking my head when I heard a light knock on my door.

"Come in."

It was Oz, gas mask slung over his shoulder (a first), looking shy and trepidatious, with Miss K leaning in behind him and beaming.

"Have a seat, Oz," I said, trying to sound like a commanding officer. "Smoke 'em if you got 'em."

He sat down but made no move to light up. I stubbed what was left of mine out.

"I have one question: how? How in the world did you do this?"

He grinned. "Well, school's out—they say it could be February before we go back—so I've been taking the #4 Bus out to the U of H library. I've long since read every book they have on criminology. But did you know you can order any library book from any library?"

"I have heard tell of such a thing."

He nodded, knowingly. "It's called an inter-library loan. I ordered a half dozen from the University of California, though I guess that could take a while with the war and all. Cal had the first Department of Criminology in the U.S., you know."

"So, these books taught you how to write reports like this?"

"Well, that and I looked at some of your old ones from the files and tried to do it the way you do. All of the words were there, I just had to figure out what order to put them in."

"Before I say anything else, I should say your report is letter perfect. I don't want to know your sources on the income tax filing or what you mean, exactly, by 'an unofficial review of naval archives,' but aside from that, I wouldn't change a damn word."

Oz was beaming now, almost as broadly as Miss K was.

"Yes, sir." He pulled out his pack and shook one out. "Thanks, Mr. Ross. I wanted it to be just right for you. Miss K made it look great," he said, looking at her with what I hoped was brotherly affection.

"I'm not kidding, Oz. God knows how many reports I've read from detectives with decades under their belt. I don't think I've seen one any better. Most were nowhere near as good. I kid you not. And having a copy of the note is invaluable."

Then he said something that endeared him to me even more. "The guys worked really hard."

I swallowed. "But here's the thing you really need to know, okay?"

His mood sobered. "Yes, sir?"

"You've found your calling in life. Years before I ever did, I might add."

A bit of the old swagger flowed back into his posture. He blew a tentative smoke ring at the ceiling. "Thanks, Mr. Ross. So, what do you know about this Branco fellow? We think he's bad news."

"He's up to no good, that much is for sure, but we have to connect him to something illegal to do anything about it."

"That seems like the hardest part. It's not enough to know in your bones that the guy is bad. We have to provide clear and convincing evidence. And it has to be the kind of evidence that will stand up in open court with a slickster defense lawyer hammering away at it."

"You learn fast, kid."

I unlocked the top drawer of my desk, where I kept the petty cash, and counted out nearly all of it.

I looked him in the eye. "The order of the day is celebration. If you were any older, I'd offer you a drink, but instead I'm giving you a much-deserved raise." I nodded toward the pile of cash. "That's to pay everybody. This," I said adding another twenty "is for expenses past and future, and *this*," another twenty went onto the stack, "is your bonus for writing the best report I've read since I don't know when. Doesn't matter whether you work for a local department or the FBI, half the job is writing reports. Hell, more than half."

"Thank you, Mr. R. That means a lot coming from you. Can we keep Branco under surveillance?"

"If you promise me you will steer clear enough of him that he doesn't catch you at it. He's a dangerous customer."

"You're the one I'm worried about. Did you know you were under surveillance?"

"I did not. But it looks like Branco's goon wasn't staking me out after I got home, so much as checking back to see if I had turned in. The question is, how is he maneuvering in the blackout without getting caught? He must have a job that allows him to be out. But don't worry. I'll be on the lookout. Thanks to you."

Oz stood up quickly, stubbing out the cigarette. "Okay, back to work, then. I've got a buddy who's a cabbie. I'm going to get him to help out. Don't worry, Mr. R., we won't let you down."

#

During the lunch hour, I did the last of the shopping for the dinner I planned to cook that night with Nalani. I had already laid in some pork and seafood from my local sources.

When I finally made it back to the office, Miss K greeted me. "There's an envelope on your desk, boss. Mrs. Ford dropped it off on her way to the boat."

Inside the envelope was a note from Tommy's Aunt Maybelle and two sheets from a writing tablet of the kind every woman I knew kept handy. The note, on a card with "Mrs. Stewart J. Ford" engraved across the top read:

Dear Mac,

While packing Tommy's books to donate them to the Friends of the Library, I discovered two journals he had been keeping for the last several years. Among the mostly personal entries were a few that related to you and to Hes Heston's murder. I thought you might benefit from reading them, so I have copied them out for you.

Tommy always admired and respected you, Mac. I didn't need the journals to tell me that. I knew it from my own correspondence with him, which was more frequent than you might imagine. After Tommy's parents died, within just a few months of one another, he and I became quite close and we stayed that way, in so far as we could half a world away. I know in my heart that wherever Tommy's spirit may now reside, he is pleased with me for sending these to you.

Sincerely,
Maybelle

I took a deep breath and began to read the first page of Maybelle's strong, legible hand.

Friday, October 24, 1941
Today, I met with Hes Heston near Lanikai, where no one would be likely to see us together. He told me he expected to wrap up "something big" within a day or so, something related to the opium trade in the Territory.
Two hours later, I got word he had been found dead of a double-barreled shotgun blast at Makapuu Point, just down the coast from where we had met. At first, I couldn't believe it, but I rode out there and found it to be all too true. There he was, or what was left of him. I've never been so shocked by a homicide. Who could possibly get the drop on Hes Heston, of all people?
I so didn't want to believe it that I took fingerprints from the body on the scene, and immediately compared them to his personnel file. They were a perfect match, of course. It seems pretty clear to me that he was killed to keep him from spilling the beans about opium in Hawaii.

There followed two journal entries, on in October and one in early November, in which it was clear that Tommy was continuing to blame himself. The first read: "I've got to solve this

Heston case and bring those responsible to justice. It's my fault he's dead."

A week later, he wrote this single line: "No police detective can maintain confidential informants if he can't keep them alive."

December 6, 1941

Met Mac for drinks and dinner at Wo Fat, to celebrate his birthday. I miss having someone like Mac as a partner. The place was packed, so we ended up eating at the bar. I found out Mac is no further along on the Heston case than I am. Less, in fact. I'm determined to find the answers and see Hes gets justice. It's the least I can do.

I still think it must be caught up in the opium trade, but I couldn't tell Mac that. I half-jokingly (but only half) told Mac I suspected Marcia. Everyone in town knew they hadn't gotten along in years, and once their daughter moved off to college on the mainland, their marriage finally came apart at the seams. Her alibi is airtight. But it's possible she hired someone to make the hit. She doesn't seem like the type, but it's amazing what people will do when really pressed. Who knows what really went on between the two of them? Still, the opium angle seems like the most promising one to me.

Thursday, December 11, 1941
The office was crazy today, mainly relating to the need to round up resident aliens on the detention lists as fast as we can. Regular police work will have to take a back seat for a while. It makes me feel dirty, arresting these people, none of whom seem like a legitimate threat.
I sent Mac a photostat of the Heston file, minus the Confidential Appendix. I shouldn't have given him even that much. Michaels would have my badge if he ever found out.
The only real lead in the Appendix is that Hes was working with us and expected to have something soon on the opium

trade. That's privileged police information that Mac is just not entitled to see.

The last entry was from the day before Tommy was killed.

Met a new contact today who says he can be helpful on all things related to opium, including the big boss known only as "The Chairman." According to him, word on the street at the time was The Chairman put a hit on Hes because Hes was getting too close. He said, "Heston was sticking his nose in The Chairman's business, so The Chairman blew it off."

The contact is an ex-con, but as Mac always used to say, when we would finger some hood for information, "No cop ever learned anything from consorting with angels."

I laid the pages aside and looked in the envelope to make certain that was all of it. I thought, *Now, Tommy, you are consorting with the angels. I bet you've learned a lot. If only you could tell me all about it.*

#

Riding to Su Ming's Laundry to pick up fresh shirts, I felt electrified and alive. Not even the traffic could sour my mood. When I finally managed to reach the Paki house, I discovered I had been paid a visit by the spirits fairy. A magnum of champagne and a bottle of Haig and Haig was carefully positioned in a shady corner near my front door. I put the bubbly (a 1938 Batisse Lancelot Les Riceys, no less) on to chill. The printed note attached read, "Best Wishes for a Happy and Healthy 1942, with my sincere compliments, Kintaro Sato."

I had no doubt that at least the scotch had been Koga's idea. It may have been the timeliest gift I ever received, because the very thought of a cotton dry mouth on New Year's Eve was enough to break a man's heart. I had tried various

local connections but came up empty. Or should I say 'dry'?
I immediately called Sato's office and thanked Koga for his
generosity, thereby making sure the whiskey had, in fact, come
from them. I didn't intend to poison myself and the woman I
loved through a rookie mistake.

Thinking it was best to pace myself, I poured a weak
scotch, filling most of the glass with soda and headed toward
the shower, dropping a record on the way. My machine would
play 33 1/3 rpm, and I had bought a big stack of transcription
disks from a radio station on the big island that changed musical
formats. They were capable of playing considerably longer than
the standard five minutes or so and worth every penny.

After a shower, I put on jeans and a work shirt, slid into a
pair of worn-out boat shoes, and went out back to check on my
imu, a distinctly Hawaiian invention for baking and steaming
most anything. Imagine a rock-lined, circular pit, a little over
three feet deep and not much bigger around, in which *kalua* pork
and *laulau* chicken had been slowly cooking since shortly after
daybreak, when I had covered it with sand to seal it all in. I had
added some *kulolo*, a dessert made from taro root that was only
good if cooked slowly and well. Everything was in order, the
smell of the meat and moistened banana and *ti* leaves seeping
subtly from the closed pit, with a hint of kiawe wood—mesquite,
as it's known on the mainland. The ancient Hawaiian method of
roasting meat beats everything else I've ever tried.

I changed into something more presentable in which to
pick up Nalani from Schofield and stuck a single gardenia with
a longer stem in a saddlebag, its white head poking out the
back. On the way out of the neighborhood, I stopped by the gate
in the fence that led onto Kapiolani Park Beach, where at 1500
hours, Sgt. Greg Hopkins had just started his shift as Sergeant
of the Guard with the Shore Patrol. Sgt. Hopkins, a trustworthy
fellow who hailed from Decatur in Alabama and had the drawl
to prove it, assured me that everything was "go" to execute our
corrupt bargain: full and unfettered access for night swimming
in exchange for two heaping plates of pork, laulau chicken, and

side dishes.

"You got it, Mac. Just be sure to get here before we go off duty at 2300. And try to stay out of sight when we drive by."

#

I had suggested to Nalani that she bring a swimsuit, and when I picked her up, she slipped off her businesslike sling back pumps and pulled a pair of braided beach sandals with cork wedges from a bag that slung over her shoulder.

She said, "I should have been a Girl Scout," cocking her eyebrow in that way that got to me. She took off her knit jacket, revealing a sleeveless shirtwaist dress that fit her perfectly in all the right places, tying the jacket around her waist. Without being asked, she jumped on behind me. The bike and I both purred all the way back to my house.

I opened the champagne and poured us each a flute of it. She gave me the eyebrow again, when I mentioned it was from Sato and Koga. I was discovering that the eyebrow had a language all its own, with various nuanced meanings. I looked forward to decoding all of them, in due time.

I said, "Let me give you the nickel tour."

"Nickel? I'm holding out for at least the dollar version."

"I'm not sure the place is big enough to warrant a dollar."

"I'm willing to be overcharged," she said, laughing.

When we reached the bedroom, she took the jacket from around her waist and hung it on a hanger in my closet. We finished the tour in the backyard, where I showed her the *imu*.

"You're kidding me. You know how to cook in an *imu*? My family has been here forever and only my uncle knows how to do that."

"Nothing quite like it."

She said, flatly, "My mother is going to love you." Then, more earnestly, "Thank you for going to all this trouble, Mac. What can I do to help?"

"Well, for starters, you can be in charge of the music, if you don't mind. Until you get tired of the job, then we can just turn on the radio. Oh, and there's "Auld Lang Syne" for the stroke of midnight."

Inside, she looked through the records, settling on the rollicking "Huesa No Ma" by Trio Matamoros, the perfect up-beat start to a celebration.

"What would you say to helping me make a fern salad?"

"You know about *Pahole* salad? On second thought, my mother won't believe you are even real."

While Nalani cut the onion (lengthwise) and cherry tomatoes (into quarters), I put water on to boil, washed the fiddlehead fern shoots, removing their fine "hairs" and began to cut them into segments about an inch-and-a-half long. When the water boiled, I blanched the shoots for about a minute, then plunged them into an ice bath to stop the cooking process. Once drained, the shoots went into a bowl with the onions and tomatoes. I quickly made a sauce from my pre-arranged bowls, using fish sauce, soy, vinegar, oil, and sugar, pouring it over the shoots and tossing it with my hands.

"Now it just needs to chill for a couple of hours."

She stood on tiptoe and kissed me, just a quick peck on the mouth. "Tonight is going to be delicious. And I'm betting dinner will be good, too," she added with an impish grin. "I'd better change the record."

From the living room, I heard first the congas and then the undulating saxophone of "Bruca Manigua" and repaired there with reinforcements of champagne in hand. Nalani was dancing slowly to the *son Cubano* masterpiece as if born to it. It was rhythmic and lyrical and, with her lissome movements, undeniably sexy.

"Antonio Rodriguez," I said, nodding toward the record player. "Blind from the age of seven. I met him once. A remarkable man. When I was stationed in New Orleans, I would take the ferry to Havana on my days off and do nothing but listen to guys like him."

"Nothing?" The eyebrow appeared in its most skeptical form.

"Well, almost nothing. You'd never know it to listen, but the words are sad—all about the miseries of loneliness. Then again, it's partly written in Spanish but whole verses are in a Nigerian dialect I can't decipher, so maybe those are the happy parts, where all is redeemed."

"I'm going to choose to believe that it all worked out in the end," she said, "No room for sadness in 1942 for me."

When the song wound down, I said, "Time to unpack the *imu*," I said.

I put on a leather apron and my thickest gloves and dug the pit out methodically, as I had learned to do from trial and lots of error. I put the meat and the *kulolo* on a table on the lanai to settle. Then, I threw some kukui nuts into one side of the *imu* and covered them with a little sand. They would roast on the retained heat and be perfect in an hour or two.

"The *kulolo* will be better in the morning when it's cooled and hardened, but it's not half bad warm."

"So, if I don't make it home tonight, I can tell my roommate I had to wait on the *kulolo* to get hard?"

"What you tell your roommate is your own business, but I promise it will be worth waiting for," I said with a wink, pouring us both more champagne.

"I'm getting tipsy, Mac."

"The swim will do us good. We can go right after dark."

"How in the world are we going to swim?"

"Oh, ye of little faith. You have to believe. In the meantime, I have a fabulous goat cheese from the big island, and some Portuguese bread I got from Peter Ochoa's family that is perfect with it. Let's have some on the lanai while we watch the sun go down, shall we? It will soak up some of the bubbles."

When we had settled in, she said, "Do all your dates run like clockwork?"

I looked pained by the question. "I'll have you know it takes weeks of planning to be this completely spontaneous."

She smiled and her big, brown eyes regarded me. She put her hand atop mine in a way that reminded me of our lunch date. We sat, not speaking, until the record began to hiss.

#

CHAPTER 10

I t was a postcard night. A silver moon, within a sliver of being full, rose above the dark green of Diamond Head, lighting up the edges of low, diaphanous clouds that marched stately by on the trade winds. The clouds were purest white on the edges nearest the moon, shading away to pink and then lavender. Higher up, fiery red mare's tails caught the last of the sun, now over the horizon.

I had loaned Nalani a flannel robe for the short ride to the beach, but we rode slowly to keep a low profile in the curfew, and to make it harder for anyone trying to follow our movements. It helped that the headlights had been painted blue, per regulation. I had checked twice to make sure my night driving pass was in my bag, along with my revolver.

We went north along Paki Avenue, just past the edge of the park—now looking like it had always been an army encampment —and took a left on Monsarrat, down to the triangle with Kalakalua, avoiding the checkpoint we would have encountered on the more direct route. As we coasted past the zoo, the Indian rumbling beneath us, we could hear a troop of monkeys nagging their monkey wives. The trolley wires made black lines across the dark blue sky.

The air was like a soft, warm blanket enveloping us, but not oppressive in any way. The trades rustled the leaves of a banyan tree as we pulled up to the gate in the beach fencing. I pushed the bike into the moon shadow of the old tree, stuffing my jacket and shirt and boots into the bags. We went quietly through the gate. To our right, a pier jutted several hundred feet into the water, clearly a place to avoid. We went left, as planned, to a little strip of sand near the natatorium. There, through the gap in the beach obstacles, we made our way to the water's edge, like school children playing hooky.

The moon was still low enough in the sky that it cast long shadows of the ancient crater. Every time I looked, it seemed to grow smaller and brighter as it climbed into the night sky. We paddled out, nearly to the groin—a series of long walls running parallel to the beach, without which there would be no beach at Waikiki. The water inside the pool it created was warm and calm and perfect for a night swim, even in December. We stood in the waist deep water and kissed.

Nalani said softly, "I never knew how much I missed coming here, day or night, until I couldn't anymore."

I nuzzled her neck and spoke quietly into her ear, reminding myself how voices carry over water, "There's nothing worse than having something wonderful, only to lose it."

I pressed my check against Nalani's and, looking up at the moon, raised my right hand and cupped its silvery outline, as if holding it back. Nalani shot me a sideways glance and without a word positioned her left hand like a bracket around the opposing limb of the moon, so that we held it captive between us. I thought of the haiku, by Basho.

We kissed some more and kanoodled like a pair of lovebirds, smiling and laughing in the warm water. I didn't see the Jeep until it was well past the pier, moving in our direction and sweeping its "God-light" back and forth across the water. There was no time to get to the beach and out the gate. I motioned for Nalani to follow, and we swam out to the groin, climbing over it and into the water just beyond, holding on to the cement wall and each other. The water here, from the open Pacific, was a good ten degrees colder, maybe more.

The light swept back and forth. A voice, improbably loud, said, "I thought I saw something, Eddie."

I whispered, "Just stay behind the wall, they'll be gone soon."

The voice, sounding a bit drunken now, said, "Is that a Jap

submarine?"

"Where?"

"Right there," the first voice said, right before a shot rang out, tearing off a chunk of seawall about twenty yards to our right.

"That's part of the wall, damnit. You're going to get us in trouble. Let's get the hell out of here, you crazy sumbitch."

By the time they had moved on, Nalani had begun to shiver. We swam for the beach, where I wrapped her in both towels, the robe, and my jacket, rubbing her arms and legs to get the blood flowing.

Her fingers traced the scar down my hip, to where it disappeared into my swim trunks. Through chattering teeth, she said, "I've always wanted to know where you got it."

"Let's get home and I'll tell you all about it."

#

"Why don't you take a nice hot shower to warm up and wash the salt off and I'll pour you a glass of champagne. Or, we have scotch."

"Scotch, please." she said. "But make it a light one."

I turned on KGMB and poured each of us a scotch and soda. She came in, wearing the robe and toweling her long dark hair.

"I thought about it in the shower," she said. "I think your buddies were just messing with you."

"Really?"

"It seems obvious."

"Wow, and it never even occurred to me. Maybe I'm in the wrong business."

"I doubt that. But maybe you need a levelheaded woman around who sees the world for how it really is."

#

We sat on the lanai, talking about the good and the bad of 1941. We talked about anything and everything. We talked through the *kalua* pork and the *laulau* chicken, with its portion of butterfish, which lived up to the name, and the *nomasu* with tiny pieces of shrimp. There are as many versions of that Japanese vinegar-dressed dish as there are cooks who make it. Mine was made with cucumbers and carrots and *daikon* and a little lime, and it proved a nice counterpoint to the richness of the pork. By the time we came to the dessert, the war and the work had receded.

I said, "I cheated and bought the *kulolo* from a family I know, so all I had to do was put it in the pit."

"You didn't have to confess. Although I might have wondered how you had time to work the taro. This is really good warm. I've never had it that way."

Nalani licked the sticky *kulolo* from the tips of her fingers. When we kissed, I could smell the caramel notes of the dessert, the terroir of the champagne, the peat of the scotch. But mostly, I drew in great draughts of Nalani Castelo, of her sandalwood and floral essence.

We never made it to the midnight toast, or "Auld Lang Syne," although we were true to its spirit of renewal and rebirth. We moved on to other songs, other dances, other stories that surpassed the ghazals of Hafez, and the stanzas of Tagore. For us, at least, the moon rested between the clouds, and all was right with the world. For what seemed the longest time, we lay entwined, in a trance of blissfulness. When, at last, I stretched to check my wristwatch on the nightstand I was amazed.

"It's not even ten-thirty," I said.

Nalani's slender fingers moved along the scar again. "I've been down this winding road a few times. I like where it takes me. But you still haven't told me how it got there."

I told her about the bar fight and how stupid I was not to just walk away. "I was full of piss and vinegar back then. Thankfully, it must be somebody's job up in heaven to look out for damned fool idiots." She pulled me close, and this time it was her finger quieting my lips.

The second *kaunu* was slower, more soulful, with less animal intensity, but more twists and turns, peaks and valleys, a diminuendo here, a series of crescendi there. We fell asleep wrapped up in each other's dreams.

#

The first hint of dawn woke me. I watched the purple light coming through the open window as it spilled across Nalani's perfect, honey-colored back, down the long valley of her spine, where it pooled in two little dimples and spilled across the sheet wrapped low on her hips. The dawn slowly brightened until the light, or perhaps the chorus of Amakihi birds, woke her.

She smiled, and I kissed her and said, "Good morning."

"I'll say," she said, with a voice still full of sleep. "How are you so chipper? Have you been up hunting a pig and making our breakfast already, my amazing man?" She reached for the nightstand, snapped off the gardenia blossom and put it behind her left ear. Its heady, sweet smell drifted across the bed.

"No, but the *kulolo* is going to be amazing."

"You are."

"How do you like your coffee?"

I saw the wheels turning, for the briefest instant, before she replied, "The same way I like my man: hot and strong, and twice before I go to work."

I was momentarily thrown off balance, a bit wide-eyed.

"Coming right up."

#

Hawaii's New Year's gift to itself was a half day off and not an hour more. By some unconscious collaboration, stores, offices, and the military government (there was no other government now, under martial law) had all settled on high noon as the time to shake off the hangover, have a little hair of the dog that bit ya, and get your ass back to winning the war.

When Nalani and I had finished not getting enough of each other, she steamed a dress that magically appeared from the Girl Scout bag, hanging it in the bathroom with the shower on hot. We got dressed and put on leis, which everyone was encouraged to do on New Year's Day, in honor of the war dead. I took Nalani to work and then came back down the King Kamehameha Highway to the University of Hawaii. I wanted to look through newspapers from the period just before the Nakajima murder, on the remote chance something helpful might stand out.

Looking at November and December editions of the *Star-Bulletin* and the *Advertiser* in such a concentrated way, I saw something that hadn't made much of an impression at the time —the sheer overconfidence of practically every establishment voice. In the articles, opinion pieces, and even official pronouncements the complacency and hubris was right there in cold, hard type.

"Why Japan is deadly afraid of the American Fleet." "Hawaii, our impenetrable fortress in the Pacific." "Where will the Japs strike? Not Hawaii." On and on, all pride before the fall.

Everyone from General Marshall to Maybelle's kindergarten pal, Frankie Knox, had made pronouncements that would embarrass them forevermore. They insisted the U.S. Navy was the most formidable fighting force the world had ever seen. "The Navy isn't going to be caught napping!"

One enthusiastic correspondent said U.S. forces on Hawaii had no cause for concern about a Japanese attack. "They know it will be a short fight, but a hot one." Strictly speaking, he was correct.

But my favorite pundit, who had never actually seen a shot fired in anger, claimed categorically, "The island of Oahu is thoroughly ringed with defenses. It would be impossible for hostile planes to come over the island." Apparently, the Japanese didn't subscribe to that paper.

There was nothing I could see that was useful to me. I made notes about the ships that came and went from the commercial harbor, in the forlorn hope the Shipping News might prove meaningful somehow. Mostly the exercise made me nostalgic for a world that was gone forever.

I decided, as long as I was there, to look back to late

October and the days preceding Hes' murder. It was no more promising. How placid, frivolous, and full of itself that world seemed, when judged from the one I now lived in.

The only thing that was notebook worthy was the report of a mysterious disappearance. A Major Roger Lawson had simply vanished. He was last seen heading out for a hike in the Aiea mountains, carrying a walking stick and wearing his khaki uniform and an old hat. No one had seen or heard from him since. It was relegated to page six—knocked off the front page by the lurid details of Hes' murder.

The story of Lawson's disappearance re-emerged, briefly, right after the attack on December 7, with newspaper speculation about whether he was a Japanese spy who got picked up by a submarine, as some insisted, or was kidnapped by Japanese forces when he stumbled onto their observation post, or signaling fires, or training camp—take your pick.

#

Back in my office, Miss Kaimani hurried out from behind her desk with a somber air and an official-looking envelope. The return address was Washington, District of Columbia. I tore it open and scanned rather than read it. It seemed I was already developing an immunity to official communications from the War Department.

"You are hereby ordered... subject to a fourteen-day activation period... in the event of such activation, you will be told where to report... and so on and so forth."

I tossed it onto my desk.

"Everything okay, boss?"

"It depends on what you mean by 'okay,' I suppose," I said, with a forced smile.

She looked pained. "I'm sorry, boss. Anyways, here's a message from Marcia Heston."

It read, "Please call when you can. I would like you to drop by, so I can show you something you need to see."

#

Most women look a little silly in culottes. Marcia Heston was the exception that proved the rule. She appeared as if she had just come from winning the ladies' club championship at 6-0, 6-1, with lingering questions as to whether she threw that one game near the end just to be gracious.

Marcia kissed my cheek and said, "I have us out by the pool, it's so lovely, but I wanted you to see this first.

She led me to the hallway, where every photograph had been restored to its rightful place, save one—leaving a single open space a little more than halfway down the right-hand wall, at eye level. Marcia picked up a stack of prints from the bow front bar at the end of the hallway and handed them to me.

"Aren't I clever? I used these old photos to figure out where everything went. It took the better part of a day."

I thumbed through them, comparing them to the scene in front of me. "Great job. They all look right to me. Even though most of them are a bit out of focus in the reference photos, you can still make out the general outlines of what's in each shot— like a blurry jigsaw puzzle."

She was proud of herself. "Yes, and sometimes I got lucky, and the background was in sharp focus, rather than the intended subject. I probably took most of those," she said, laughing.

"So, what about the missing one. Is this the best image you have of it?"

"Yeah, that's where my luck ran out. But you can tell it's four figures, almost certainly males, judging by the length of the hair. All dressed similarly."

"I agree. Still, not much to go on. Any ideas?"

Marcia said, "I think it had to be from Hes' fraternity days. All the photos around it are from that period." She looked at the restored photographs as if they were from someone else's life and gave a slight shutter. "Do you mind if we go outside. This hallways gives me the morbs now."

On a table on the pool deck, Marcia had laid out Hawaii's

version of *charcuterie*: an assortment of cheeses, nuts, and pineapple. So far, it seemed Marcia Heston had made a bigger dent in the war than it had made in her.

Marcia said, "What's scary is thinking that whoever broke in here might have been someone close enough to us to have been in that photo."

"And scarier still when you think that whoever killed Hes might be in it."

"I thought of that, too. But I didn't want to go there in my mind."

"Here's something you can do. Check with all of your friends who have taken photographs at your house. There must be plenty of camera bugs in your circle."

She brightened. "Of course! Why didn't I think of that? That should give us dozens more to work with."

I thought it best to leave it at that, for now. "Great pineapple," I said to take her mind off the subject. "Somehow it never gets old."

"I've always loved pineapple, but Hes never would let me serve it, you know. He said, with pineapple growing as far as the eye could see, it was crass. How many times must I have bitten my tongue when he said, 'That would be like serving shave ice in the arctic'?"

I shook my head. "He was always a bit predatory in conversation."

"He would have considered that a compliment, but then you know that as well as I."

"You're right. He did enjoy having that reputation. What was that sign he had on the pool?" I looked along the fence. 'Beware of the Shark?' I don't see it now, but it was on the fence as far back as I can remember."

"I bet Hernando took it down. He didn't care for it any more than I did. Talk about crass. Who refers to himself as a shark? To think I let that man lecture me on anything! My mother always told us, 'Never speak ill of the dead,' but dammit, Mac."

"I know. He could be a pill. No sense pretending otherwise, just because he went and got himself killed."

Marcia nodded and sighed, "Not at our age." She raised her glass. "The shark is gone. Long live the fish!"

#

On my way out of the neighborhood, I saw an old black Packard sitting at a curb, the driver mostly hidden behind a Michelin guide. It stuck out like a sore thumb. Was I up against the Keystone Krooks? But, when I came even with it, the guide came down, revealing a revolver. A man with dark curly hair pointed it at me. I gunned the bike so hard the front wheel came off the pavement, then heard the shot. The hair on the back of my neck stood to attention. The car swung out behind me.

I zigged and zagged, sped up and slowed down, heading in the general direction of Chinatown. After the first couple of blocks, it wasn't a fair fight. Right on Chaplain, quick left on Smith. Left on Bishop, right on Merchant. Tin Can Alley, Blood Town, Mosquito Flats, even the notorious Hell's Half Acre had all been on my beat at one time or another before I reached the rank of Detective. The saying was there were three hundred ways into the Acre, but four hundred ways out. I used some of the tighter ones to put plenty of room between me and the black Packard.

There was no way he could keep up without a motorbike. I pulled the bike down an alley off Fort Street, stashing it behind a gaggle of garbage cans. The sharp, sweet smell of dry cleaning fluid was in the air. I went around to the front door of China Luck Cleaners and up to the desk. A sign read, "Please ring bell," so I did.

An older, Chinese gentleman in a Manchu shirt presented himself and, in impeccable English, said "How may I help you, sir?"

"I need to leave a message, please. For Doctor Quong."

He gave the slightest hint of a smile. "Of course, sir."

I wrote on a page of my notebook and tore it out. "Shot at by man believed to be Branco "Money" Moses. Please arrange for counter-surveillance of my movements if you are not already doing so. Will be at my office within two hours. Planning not to turn Moses over to HPD, in hopes he will lead us to bigger fish." I signed it and wrote the time.

"May I trouble you for an envelope, please sir?"

"Yes, sir. One moment, please." He disappeared through the curtain behind the desk and quickly returned with a standard business envelope, with the name and return address of the establishment in English and Japanese, reflecting the makeup of its clientele. The Japanese had been stricken through with a dark, black marker, but you could still make out the ideograms.

I put the note in the envelope, sealed it, and wrote "Doctor Quong" in large letters on the front. The gentleman took the note and bowed, backing out through the curtain.

#

I could never get used to being shot at, so I figured while I was in the neighborhood, I would pay a visit to The Blue Lagoon and have a little something to settle my nerves. After a couple, I felt remarkably better, so I rode over to my old unit, Naval Intelligence, to see what they knew about the disappearance of Roger Lawson.

It quickly became clear that the current occupants of the office didn't have much regard for my prior service there. The Deputy Director fobbed me off on the Second Assistant Deputy Director, who looked like he had just won Most Likely to Succeed at his junior high. But that too didn't matter, because so little was officially known about the subject I had come to discuss that I could have gotten every bit of it from the janitor, in between squeezes of the mop in the already spotless corridor.

The young commander said, "I'm afraid we know next to nothing about Major Lawson's disappearance, Mr. Ross. One minute he was driving off to go hiking in the mountains, as was his habit, the next minute he was gone."

I was struck by his flair for the dramatic, not a good trait

GUYMCCULLOUGH

for intelligence work. "That's it?"

To his credit, he never looked at the contents of the file. "There was a portion of a khaki shirt found in mid-November, near one of the trails the major frequented. It did have human blood on it," he said in a disapproving voice, as if the blood or whoever left it had personally let him down, "but I'm sure I do not have to tell you, of all people, Mr. Ross, how inconclusive that is."

"No. No, Commander, you don't. I'm assuming you talked to his friends, colleagues, enquiring into his mental state, his finances, that sort of thing."

"Yes, sir. I'm not at liberty to go into any of the details. We did use tracking dogs, but they couldn't pick up anything on the trail he was believed to have taken. I can tell you that a number of interviews were conducted. He even left a diary, though it was not very illuminating to anyone other than an entomologist, or perhaps a sea captain. But, not-so-long story short, we have absolutely zero indication that Major Lawson took his own life by throwing himself off a cliff in Aiea." His certitude reminded me of the categorical statements from the newspaper articles.

I stood and offered my hand. "Thank you for your time, Commander." I gave him a card and the usual spiel about calling, but we both knew it was all Kabuki theatre. To prove it, he very thoughtfully walked me back out to the lobby.

#

Bing Edwards was waiting for me in my outer office. As I showed him into mine, Miss K made an ugly face to his back.

"Come in, Bing. I'd offer you a drink, but I don't have anything stronger than coffee."

"Not our fault, Mac. You can thank the Army for that. They can't make up their mind about what fucking day it is. You wouldn't believe the number of calls we're getting these days about rummies with the D.T.s, all because they won't re-open the whiskey stores."

"Oh, I bet I would. You're forgetting I was a beat cop in the early days of the Depression."

146

He had quit listening. "And now the stills have cranked up, although that's the Sheriff's problem," he said, with considerable relief. "Mostly."

"How can I help you, Bing?"

"I came to do you a favor. To offer you a job," he said. "We have so many background checks to run we need half a dozen more guys. You'd be contract labor, with nobody to answer to but me. Safe, simple, and lucrative as hell."

"As easy as that, huh?"

"Yep, easy peasy."

"Would I still be able to work on my own cases?"

He shifted in his chair, which rendered his answer redundant. "No, this would be a full-time operation. You can't mix official and unofficial business."

"I see. I thank you, buddy, but I'm not interested."

"Ah, come on, Mac. Think it over. Sleep on it, for Christ's sake."

"I don't need to sleep on it. I can't just abandon what I'm working on."

"The Nakajima case?"

"Well, that and a few other things."

"What other things? I'm trying to double your income, buddy."

"This and that."

Alright," he said, rising to his feet. "Don't say I didn't try, Mac."

I saw him out the door. When I came back, the phone rang.

"Mac Ross, confidential investigations."

"Mr. Ross, it's Oz. Osvaldo. I've been tailing Branco this afternoon and I'm out here at Schofield watching him just sitting in his car. It's like he's waiting for someone to come out, so he can follow them."

"I don't want to know how you got past the front gate. How long has Branco been there?"

"A little over thirty minutes."

"Where exactly?"

"In a parking lot at one niner four niner Humphrey's Road." My heart skipped a beat. It was Nalani's office

"The headquarters for the 24th Infantry Division?"

"There are all kinds of offices in there, but I believe so. I'm at a phone booth around the corner, so I can't see the sign from here."

"Big building in the shape of an 'L'?"

"Yes, sir, that's the one."

"Listen carefully, Oz. I want you to go into the building and ask for the officer of the day. Tell him you work for me, and we have reason to believe Nalani Castelo may be in danger. Stay there with her until either I or Peter Ochoa get there. If it's Peter, make sure they go out the back way, got it?"

"Got it, Mr. Ross. I'm going in."

I called Peter Ochoa at his home on the North Shore. After about twenty rings, I hung up and rifled through my address book for the number at the North Shore Surf Club. Peter and his guys were organizing efforts to clear the beaches of kiawe, to free up fields of fire, in case of a Japanese landing. They based themselves out of our club house. Before I could find the number, the phone rang.

"Mac Ross."

A voice muffled by a towel or blanket, said, "If you want Miss Nalani to be safe, lay off the Nakajima case. You don't get no more warnings, bub."

"Listen here you son of a bitch. If you lay so much as a finger on her, I will fucking kill you." I realized I was now standing and shouting into a dead phone line.

Miss K. stuck her head cautiously around the door, her eyes the size of headlights.

"You okay, boss?"

I nodded and dialed the phone. Peter answered the phone at the surf club on the first ring.

"Listen up, buddy. I need your help."

"What's up?"

"I need you to pick up Nalani Castelo from work at Schofield. Her office is in the HQ of the 24th Infantry Division. One nine four nine Humphrey's Road."

"I know the place."

"There's a thug named Moses Branco who is sitting in her parking lot. I just had a call threatening harm to her if I don't give up the Nakajima case."

"The bastards."

"You can reach her well before I can. Take her out the back way and get her to my beach shack until I can get there, will you? You'll need to be armed. And can you get the guys together?"

"Yeah, sure, we're all here clearing *Kiawe* on the beach."

"Tell them to bring their rifles and plenty of ammunition. How many flares do we have there at the club?"

"Hold the line," he said, sitting down the phone and quickly returning. "Six."

"Have the guys form a perimeter. Branco and his boys will probably wait for dark. Tell them if anything moves to fire off a flare. If it's clearly not a friendly, shoot if they have a clean shot."

"You got it, Mac," he said, his voice at last betraying excitement.

"I'd like you to stay with Nalani at my place. Tell the guys to be careful not to let them outflank you to the beach. And don't get silhouetted against the beach at sunset. You'll be an easy target."

"I'll tell them, but they know how to do."

"I'm at my office. I'll be there in thirty minutes."

"You can't get there in thirty minutes, but we will be waiting for you, Mac."

"Like hell I can't."

I grabbed the only gun I had at the office, a big Webley that dated to the Great War, ran down the stairs three at a time, and jumped on the bike. I tore through town, darting in and out of traffic, taking the shoulder when I had to, and considering the sidewalk more than once, ever conscious of the passing of time.

Once out of town, I opened it up. Plumeria leaves swirled behind me in elaborate eddies as I sped through them.

King Kamehameha Highway wound from the city through cane and sugar plantations to the North Shore. The pilots at Wheeler raced their sports cars along it all the time, from the base to the ocean. One would honk their horn at another and off they both would go, hell for leather. I kept thinking about where I would put the bike if I encountered a couple of them coming around a bend but didn't let it slow me down.

Mostly, I had the road to myself and my desperate thoughts about what might happen to Nalani if I couldn't get to her before the thugs did. But some level of my mind must have still been paying close attention to the road.

I was just past the turn-off to Route 801, in a desolate stretch of green fields bordered by scrub and telephone poles, where the red dirt and the fecund smell of the cane come right up to the roadway. If I had been a minute earlier, or a minute later, things would not have aligned as they did. It took the sun being at just the right angle. I saw, from left to right, the briefest flash of horizontal light. I knew instantly it was a length of piano wire stretched across my path at head height, an old and crude trick. My first thought was to lay the bike down and try to get on top of it. But, in the same instant, I knew that wouldn't work. Whoever placed the wire would simply step out of the cane field and shoot me dead.

They say your life flashes before your eyes and it's true. My eyes saw a three-year-old at an orphanage. A fight with a bully in grammar school. Discovering the one adult who saw something in me. Taking the oath in the Navy.

The answer came to me before I could take the next breath. I threw the throttle hand forward, slowing briefly, waited until the last possible instant, then cranked the throttle full. The front wheel rose, cutting the wire with the metal chassis of the bike. I heard a loud, high-pitched twang. The cowling on my rear wheel came off and clattered away.

When the front wheel hit the ground, I began making evasive moves, left and right, varying my speed ever so slightly. They got off three shots before I accelerated through the next turn and out of their line of fire. The closest one I saw kicked up dust just ahead of me and to my right. But it wouldn't take them long to get their car, probably stashed just up 801, and come after me.

The threat to Nalani had been a ruse designed to get me going fast down through the valley, where they could kill me and toss me into a cane field. I had swallowed the bait, like an idiot, which meant I had brought her closer to danger by asking Peter to take her to the beach house.

I came tearing up to the shack, dirt and sand flying. I noticed with approval that Peter had already opened the door to the storage shed, so no one could pop out of it when we least expected it. I also took in the fact that Peter and his crew had removed a lot of the brush on this end of the beach since the last time I had seen it. That meant a lot less cover on the approaches to the shack.

Peter threw open the door and I took the bike up the steps and into the cottage. Maybe they would think I had kept on going up the coast. Nalani stepped into the room, and we embraced. Peter shook my hand, as calmly as if we were going surf fishing.

He said, "What happened to your jacket, Mac?"

I looked at my leather jacket. It had been cut completely through on the right side when the thin wire parted and whipped back across the roadway. Another couple of inches would have sliced my liver in half.

#

By nightfall, we had moved the refrigerator and two heavy chests into the bathroom to create a safe zone. Eventually, whoever had tried to behead me would get close enough to the cottage to just fire into it, and the frame shack was no match for high-caliber rounds. At least the bathtub and the tile and these heavy pieces would improve the odds. I made Nalani promise, no matter what happened, not to get out of the bathtub.

Peter and I each took one of the two larger windows, giving us a line of fire on three sides of the building. There was no way in on the remaining side. With a jolt of fear, I wondered whether they were smart enough to try burning us out from the blind side. They could siphon enough gas from the Packard if they thought it through.

We first saw them as the last of the light began to fade, around seven. We counted three of them. They would have to make quick work of it. The full moon had already risen, and even though it was barely above the horizon, it would soon become a factor in our favor.

I whispered across to Peter, "I hope like hell the guys are in place."

All Peter said was, "Count on it."

"I am. Otherwise, our goose is cooked."

"Goose is not on the menu tonight, Mac. Only goon."

The laughter cut the tension and we settled in, allowing our eyes to adjust to the fading light and watching for the slightest sign of movement.

We heard a familiar 'Pop', and a flare soared into the air, then slowly descended in its tiny parachute, the flickering arc-light brilliance of it swinging back and forth, alternately lengthening and shortening the shadows of the house, and the shed, and the trees. It took almost a minute for the flare to burn out, leaving us a little night blind. At least the goons would have the same problem.

"Bandit at my one o'clock, incoming," Peter whispered and squeezed off a shot. May as well let them know it wasn't going to be a cakewalk. Maybe they didn't want to get shot at today, for some reason.

Pop, the flare lit up the scene without warning, followed quickly by a rifle shot.

"He got the bastard," Peter said quietly.

"That's cutting them down to size."

To my right, I saw someone moving toward the shack

from behind tree cover. There was too much of it over there for comfort. I fired off a round, just to keep him pinned down as long as possible. By now, it must have dawned on our attackers that the flares were not coming from us, which would tend to upset their calculations. The moon had risen higher. As expected, they began firing left and right into the cottage.

The next flare revealed a man scurrying into position to the left, along with a half dozen holes in the walls, where rounds had already penetrated. The light from the flare shone through them like tiny flashlights. They looked to be about the size of a .45.

We couldn't keep this up much longer. With the gunmen this close, our squad couldn't fire at them without running a very real risk of taking one of us out. I called softly to Nalani and met her at the bathroom door. In a quiet voice, I explained to her and to Peter what I had in mind, giving each of them a set of steps to follow.

I wrestled the speaker for the record player up and onto the windowsill in the living room, and set the first record on the stack spinning, with the tone arm in the up position, hovering over the disk. I cranked the volume all the way up and glanced at the record as it rotated: Jelly Roll Morton's "Billy Goat Stomp." Perfect.

I retrieved a blanket from the bedroom.

"Wrap this around the bike while I crank it."

I climbed onto the Indian and gently kicked the starter. It purred quietly—Rocinante chomping at the bit. If this didn't work, it would certainly qualify as a quixotic gesture, but chances are I wouldn't be around to worry about it. In the end, I concluded, it was the only play available to us.

Peter stood by the door. I put the Webley in my right hand, wrapped my left around the throttle, thanking the gods it was an Indian with its unusual design, and nodded to Peter and then Nalani. She scurried across and kissed me, whispering, "I love you. Please be careful," then moved quickly back to the phonograph. I thought, *Just don't ride straight at them, or straight away from them, and they'll never be able to hit you.*

"Okay, on my count. Three. Two. One."

On the count of One, Peter swung the door open quickly and smoothly.

Nalani let the tone arm fall. I gunned the Indian and roared through the open door, just as the first deafening bleat of a goat boomed from the big speaker. It was followed immediately by a flare—Pop. Whoever was manning the flares was heads up.

As I came down the steps into the artificial light of the flare, I saw a man behind the shrubs to my left. He stood up and instinctively pulled away from the blast of sound. Jelly Roll and his band joined in, and I brought the Webley up. The gun roared and the dark shape fell into its own shadow.

To my right, behind the shed, I could just make out the right shoulder of the other gunman. I drove the bike forward quickly, at an angle to him. A round blew a huge splinter from the wall of the shed. Peter, providing cover fire.

The flare swung like a drunken pendulum, fast then slow, then fast again, falling toward the earth and beginning to fizzle. Behind the shed, the man, lit from above, grew small and insignificant. *Wait for it.* I was nearly close enough to have a shot when, unable to stand it, he looked around the corner.

Peter and I fired at the same instant, the sounds merging with one another. We hit him twice in quick succession, making his body twitch in a little dance that reminded me of revelers in New Orleans, doing something they call the voodoo dance, flailing rapidly with demented force. He fell just as the flare went out.

I turned hard left and sped directly toward the first man, gun aimed. I saw him move and fired. He didn't move anymore. I skidded up to the body and kicked his gun away. He was dead. Peter came running out of the house. Another flare went up and I used the light to race back to the man behind the shed. He had taken one through the head and one through the heart. *Was there a fourth man, somewhere in the darkness?*

In the light of the sixth and last flare, Pederson, Grimes, Tanaka, Arando and Edward Ferrer walked out of the bushes, until they were wrapping their arms around us. I got off the bike, legs trembling, and ran inside the house. As I went through the door, Nalani came into the kitchen, a look of horror on her face.

"It's okay," I said, pulling her to me. "We're all okay."

#

When we tried to call the Sheriff, we discovered the phone line had been cut. Pederson volunteered to run to his house and call them.

"Next, call the FBI," I said. "I'll write down the number. Tell whoever answers that I am bringing a witness to a homicide to them, for protective custody, as fast as I can get there from the North Shore."

Down the road, we found the old Packard, with the registration card on the steering wheel—Moses Branco. Oz would be happy to know we got our man. It took me almost two hours to get downtown to Rogers' office and then back to the North Shore to meet up with the Sheriff and sign a statement.

When I got back to the cottage, several deputies and the Shore Patrol were talking quietly with the guys. The patrol had seen the flares and decided they would be missing out if they didn't get in on whatever was afoot. It occurred to me that we were lucky they took their time in getting there. It would have been downright awkward if they had walked into our firefight.

Grimes pulled up in a pickup truck. His last mission had been to fetch some homebrew hooch. Oz's uncle handed me a coconut full of the rankest stuff. But I drank every last drop of it and slept like it was my birthday, knowing Nalani was safe for the night.

#

CHAPTER 11

The only safe arrangement was for Nalani to stay with me at the Paki Avenue house. There was no way in hell Money Branco was at the top of this particular pyramid of thuggery. Whoever hired Branco and his cronies was still out there, and I doubt he had lost his enthusiasm for making sure I wasn't around to work on the Nakajima case. Or was it the Heston case they wanted me off? I was beginning to think it was all one case.

Waking up that first morning, I lay still and grinned like the village idiot for a good five minutes. It was one of the best moments of my life. She seemed equally happy with the arrangement and our harmony. It may be from sheer laziness on my part, but I've never been able to live with anyone who wasn't easy to get along with. So, it was gratifying to see that each of us felt an ease right from the first day and night. She made everything fun. The day to day reality was just as delightful, just as tinged with excitement and electricity, as New Year's Eve had been.

I made coffee and took her a steaming cup, strong and hot. She murmured a thank you and gave me a half-lidded kiss.

"I have a meeting with Warren Sears this morning, so headed to shower."

"Leave it running. I'll come right behind you," she said, padding off to the kitchen in one of my long sleeve shirts.

The water reminded me of the dream I'd had, toward morning. I saw Daniel Nakajima, pale and deathly. He was swimming off a verdant coast. Sharks circled him, their fins like submarine conning towers. But instead of coming in out of the water, Daniel kept swimming out to sea. Even before the sharks closed in, he had begun to drown. I had awakened with a start, gasping for air, as if I had been the one breathing in lungfuls of saltwater.

I let the warm shower water run over me. *What must it mean?* Maybe I should ask Nalani. Her Mother was, after all, a seer. Then, I realized where else I had known Daniel to be swimming. I turned off the water, wrapped a towel around me without drying off, and went in search of my briefcase. The Nakajima file had grown considerably larger. I flipped to the letters Daniel had written to his girlfriend, Keiko, and there it was.

I do enjoy walking down to the beach for a morning swim. I can't do that every day on Oahu.

Daniel had not seen anyone he knew in Lihue or Eleele, but what about on his morning swim? Or on the way to or from the beach?

I found the phonebook and looked up Reid's Aerial Photography. I had used Chip Reid's outfit to create exhibits showing the real estate holdings old Joe Hanover had tried to conceal to avoid a fair settlement with his wife, my client, Elizabeth. Warren Sears had held Chip's photographs up, one by one, until Joe's lawyers asked for a short recess and settled the whole thing. I called Chip and arranged to see images of Eleele, Kauai and the adjacent waters.

Next, I called the service for my messages. I had one from a nice young lieutenant I'd been working with at the Ninety-Second Maneuver Area Command. I still hoped to interview Daniel's uncle in person. But hitching a ride on the Navy's ferry, the same boat whose captain I had questioned, and the same one Daniel had taken to and from Kauai, was turning out to be every bit as tough as the captain had suggested.

Everything had been rocking along nicely, until I had submitted the form stating the reason for my travel: "to investigate the murder of Daniel Nakajima." At that point, the wheels at the Navy had slowed perceptibly and were now clanging to a halt with the message: "All civilian travel on inter-island ferries is currently suspended, pending a review. Will be in touch once we know more." In other words, 'don't call us; we'll call you.' That's what I get for telling the truth on a military form.

#

At Warren Sears' office, the news was worse.

"Thanks for coming by, Mac. I didn't want to talk about this on the phone. I'm sorry to report that Vassar, excuse me, Miss Berry I should say, has been roughed up, and thrown in jail."

"How, by whom?"

"Mostly by Bing Williams, so far as I can tell" he said, holding up an affidavit. "This is her account of it. I'll save you the trouble of reading. She was at The Bronx, after curfew, sitting at a table downstairs in her red silk pajamas, minding her own business, when Bing and a couple of boys from Vice showed up."

"That son of a bitch."

"She says he began cursing at her and saying how dare she thumb her whore nose at the law and the chief and the department. He had apparently had quite a bit to drink and so had his goons. When she tried to leave, they wouldn't let her, and when she stood up to them, he beat her up, Mac. Slapped her around, threw her against a wall, knocked her down and even kicked her once in the ribs, cracking one. They treated and released her at the hospital."

I had come out of the chair and was pacing. "So, they threw her in the city jail."

"Yes, but not before I got photographs at the emergency room. They charged her with resisting a police officer, assault and battery of a police office, and profanity. We may have to plead guilty to that last one," he said, with a half-hearted laugh.

It broke the tension enough that some reason returned, and I quit fantasizing about walking into HPD and putting a couple of rounds in Bing Williams.

"What can I do to help?"

"Help me find a taxi driver. He had just dropped off some luggage Miss Berry had sent over because they're getting ready to re-open at the Bronx. She says the cabbie saw and heard it all."

"So, find him and get a sworn statement from him. Do we have his name?"

"Yeah, it was Tommy Two-Toes. You know him."

"Everybody does. He shouldn't be too hard to find, even if he doesn't want to be."

"If I can get good statements from him to go with my photographs, they'll drop the charges, or my name isn't Buck Rogers."

"But your name *isn't* Buck Rogers."

"It's a figure of speech, Mac."

"So, they drop the charges, but no consequences for Bing?"

"We have to take our minor victories wherever we can get them."

"Alright. I'll get on it."

#

Chip Reid had the prints I needed ready for me. We easily located the little plantation houses, in two half circles, arranged around the washhouse and tea house. Tracing the route from the plantation directly to the beach, about a third of a mile, we saw it led along a dusty trail and past a single building: a cottage with a small swimming pool.

Chip gave me the prints and I gave him, over his objections, some of Sato's money.

"Mac, I hate to admit it, but I'm getting rich flying so much for the Army and Navy. I don't need your money."

"It's my client's money, and he needs it even less than you do, trust me, Chip. One day, when it is my money, I may ask a favor of you."

"Just say the word, Mac."

#

Back at the office, I called Bing Williams. Ten minutes later, he called me back.

"Change your mind, old man?"

"Bing, I want to make it clear that this call is not related to anything that has taken place in the past. I know you are a witness in the criminal prosecution of Kathleen Berry."

"Yeah, that smart ass whore needs to learn her place."

"And I want to make sure you understand that I am not attempting to intimidate you in any way or influence your testimony in that proceeding. What I am about to say relates only to the future, got it?"

"The future," he repeated, uncertainly.

"If I ever hear about you hitting Miss Berry, or any other woman, ever again, I'll be coming to pay you a visit. Understood?"

"Hey, you can't threaten a police officer. I'll—"

I hung up the phone. My hand shook a little as I lit a cigarette and smoked most of it before making my next call, to FBI Agent Jack Rogers' office. His assistant came back to the phone.

"He says come now, but you'll have to bring your own sandwich."

#

When I was shown into his office, Jack was, indeed, eating a BLT, along with what looked to be a Korean dish of pickled vegetables. I began by thanking him for looking out for Nalani while I explained three dead bodies to the sheriff.

"Now, here I am again, needing your help."

"What's up, Mac?"

"I've been trying to arrange passage on the *Charon*, the inter-island ferry to Kauai. I'll spare you the details, but the Navy was cooperating nicely until they discovered the murder I was investigating had a Japanese victim."

"Those guys are all from the mainland, they don't understand how things are on Oahu."

"Anyway, the Navy just operates the *Charon*. They don't decide who, and what, gets to ride on it. If you can get me and my bike on that boat, they'll never know or care."

Rogers put down his sandwich. "I can and I will."

"Thank you, Jack. I have a lead I really need to follow up on."

He pressed the intercom and asked his assistant to call the Harbor Master and get the departure time for the *Charon*. The assistant scurried in shortly with a slip of paper and placed it in front of him.

"Well, Mac, she sails tomorrow morning at 0700, a most uncivilized hour for starting work in our town. But it gives me time to get somebody at CINCPAC's signature on it. You'll have to get an early start. But that means, with any luck, you can get your business done and get back tomorrow night.

#

The next morning at 0645, I rolled the bike up the gangplank of the *Charon*, found an out of the way place to put it and lashed it down until all was shipshape. Then I went belowdecks and found the wardroom. It smelled of diesel and bilgewater, but would do nicely. I spread my papers out across the table. For the next several hours, I went back through every piece of paper and photostat in the Nakajima and Heston files, including the notes from my visits with Marcia. The whole kit and kaboodle, as Tommy would have said, may he rest in peace.

It's amazing what you can do when you have that much uninterrupted time to do nothing but think. Solving a case is something like catching and riding a wave—timing and method are everything. It had certainly taken me long enough to catch this one.

After steaming for almost five hours, we docked at Lihue, the only place on Kauai with what you could call a harbor. I thanked the captain, who responded with a curt nod, as if he felt uncomfortable acknowledging my presence on his vessel. I rolled the Indian down the ramp, cranked it, and set off toward the cable office.

At Western Union, I used the pay phone to call Marcia Heston.

I said, "I've got two quick questions for you."

"Fire away."

"Did Hes know a fellow named Roger Lawson, an Army Major?"

"You mean the poor fellow who disappeared in the mountains? Yes, since college."

"Had they stayed in touch?"

"They were never what I would call close, but Lawson came to parties at the house every now and then."

"When we hang up, I want you to check the photographs and see if there are any with him in it. Just call my service and leave a message. When I get back to Oahu, I'd like to come see them, if there are any. I may need to make prints."

"Of course, Mac."

"My second question is going to sound crazy."

"You forget I was married to a detective for twenty years."

"Did Hes not want you to serve pineapple because he found it too boorish for words, or because he didn't like to eat it?"

She laughed. "Both, actually. It wasn't the taste he didn't like. He liked pineapple juice fine, but he loathed the texture of the fruit. He said it set his teeth on edge."

"Thanks, Marcia. You've told me what I needed to know. I'll be in touch."

"Okay, Mac. Whatever it is you're doing, be careful."

#

Kauai is called 'the garden island,' and it has an earthy, vegetable smell that's impossible to describe, a mix of fresh greenness, pavement after a rain, flowers, saltwater, and hot sand. I had studied Chip's aerial photos and so I found the plantation without having to consult the road map. Soon, I was sitting down to tea with Daniel's uncle, who looked like a slightly shorter, heavily wrinkled version of Daniel. His friend, the plantation supervisor, served as our translator. The supervisor's English was solid, but the uncle had nothing new to offer. I confirmed that Daniel had seen no one he knew in Lihue, or on his brief shopping trip to Eleele.

"What about when he went swimming in the mornings? Did he mention seeing anything then?"

After the translation, the uncle shook his head, clearly saddened to be so unhelpful.

"Daniel told his girlfriend that he thought he had seen a ghost while he was at the plantation. Did he mention that to you?"

"No, sir. But we've always had ghosts on the plantation. I've seen them many times, ever since I was a little boy." The supervisor nodded, innocently, as if ghosts didn't bear mentioning. For a moment, I could see them as young boys, when the wood of the plantation houses was still green, and all the trees were shorter.

#

I had the supervisor show me the path Daniel would have taken to the beach. I could have easily walked it, but I wanted the bike close at hand. I found the dirt trail just before the Hanapepe River. I rode slowly, heading inland, or *makai* as we say in the islands, looking for the turnoff for the beach. There wasn't a human in sight. The only sounds were of birds and insects and the pounding surf in the middle distance, which I felt as much as heard.

The whole area was so wild and overgrown I almost missed the rickety wooden gate. I turned the bike off and wheeled it into a tight stand of ironwood trees, where it would be hidden from the road. I circled wide of the gate, in case it was being watched, and worked my way slowly toward the isolated house.

Through a gap in the trees, I could see the low bungalow with a small lanai, next to a tiny pool. I thought about coming back under cover of darkness, but I would play hell stumbling through the undergrowth without showing a light, and it would require staying overnight. If the whole thing was one big snipe hunt, I'd feel like an idiot.

I stopped under cover of the trees that surrounded the place and peered at the bungalow for signs of life. I didn't see anything of interest at first. Then, as I edged closer, my heart gave a lurch at the sight of a familiar sign: 'Beware of the Shark."

For a few minutes, I watched and waited, in the vain hope that he would come strolling up the narrow path and make it easy for me. When, after a time, no one did, I crouched low and crept up the path.

Ahead of me, nearer the house, the path broadened out, not exactly onto a lawn, but a clearing of sorts. If I could get past the chokepoint without being seen, there should be better lines of approach and a bit of cover to be had among the mango trees. I crept forward, slowly. No need to rush. I paused, then darted through the confined space between the trees.

Suddenly, I was falling, plunging into a black pit.

I landed hard, twisting an ankle. I cursed my utter stupidity. I had walked straight into a tiger trap. It was at least ten feet deep, with sides that sloped outward toward the bottom, in an inverted V-shape, making it impossible for even a cat to climb out of. It was cunningly made and cleverly concealed, but I could kick myself for being trapped by such a simple device. I suspected, however, that someone would be along soon to kick my ass for me.

For an hour or more, the only sound was the whine of mosquitoes and the occasional warbling of a house finch. The birdsong sounded like an elaborately phrased interrogatory. He kept asking me how I could be so stupid, so stupid, so STU-pid. I would have gladly given him an answer if I had one. But then, the answer was right there in the question.

Like me, the house finch was not indigenous to Hawaii. It had come relatively recently. But it would die here, and now, it seemed, so would I. Funny what goes through your head when you're looking up at the sky from a tiger pit.

I had begun to think the house might no longer be occupied, and that slow dehydration would be the death of me, when a rustling announced that someone was coming down the path.

The rustling grew louder, then stopped. There, peering cautiously over the edge of the pit, and very much alive, was William Beauclerc Heston, III. A shotgun, broken open, was draped over his left arm.

"The general who wins the battle makes many calculations before the battle is fought," he said, smiling down at me. "The general who loses makes but few calculations beforehand. Sun Zu. You forgot to make your calculations, Mac."

"Oh, we've made our calculations," I said, bluffing. It did make him glance around.

"Turn around and turn out your pockets, so I can make sure you aren't armed, although I never could get you to carry a piece

I complied. Once he saw I wasn't armed, he stood up, and gave me a smirk. "Long time, no see, Mac. What brings you out my way, partner?"

"I've come to take you back, Hes, for the murders of Roger Lawson, Daniel Nakajima, and Tommy Ford. It's time you answered for all the grief you've caused."

He laughed. "Grief? What do you know about grief?"

"A lot. I've been taking a crash course lately."

"I'll tell you about grief, old man, real grief. Grief is knowing that you're trapped in a life that's a living hell, while a whole new life, a new paradise awaits you."

"All it's gotten you so far is purgatory. You gave up paradise, for this? You had everything you wanted or needed. And if you wanted out, all you had to do was tell Marcia. She wasn't any happier than you were. She would have gladly given you a divorce."

"Well, it wasn't quite that simple, partner."

"I'm not your partner."

"A divorce wasn't the issue," he said. "Marcia wasn't the

issue. I was in too deep on too many fronts. And once I crossed The Chairman, there was no going back."

I swatted at the mosquitoes. "Get me out of here, and we'll talk about it. I know you were mixed up in the opium trade. Maybe I can help."

"Help? You? You have no idea what a ruthless bastard The Chairman is. It was all sweetness and light at first. But it's just an act. Next thing I knew, my ass was in a crack," he said, with a bitter laugh. "So, I held on to a few hundred grand I was supposed to be laundering with Chan Ho, to buy a new life."

"I can help you."

"You're in a tiger pit, asshole."

"Let me out and I'll help you, Hes."

He was no longer listening. "I had it all planned, see. Assets transferred from Frisco banks to a couple of discreet bankers in Australia and New Zealand—enough to live on for the rest of my life. And the very fucking day I'm ready to skip out, the damn Japs come calling. Now I can't take a boat or a shit without worrying someone is watching." He looked around him, as if seeing where he had ended up for the first time, the shotgun swinging on his arm. "So, here I am. Stuck in this shithole."

If I couldn't convince him, my only hope was to stall. "Come on, man, it can still work out. Let me help you."

"You're so naïve, Mac. You always were," he said, with real disappointment in his voice. "Now that The Chairman knows I had planned to skip out on him, there's no way out for Hes Heston. I have to be somebody else now. He was going to kill me, so I beat him to it by killing myself."

"You're going to do all that only to let the Territory hang you? I can help you get away."

That didn't seem to sit well with him. I had just reminded him that I had enough on him to put him away. The finches warbled at me disapprovingly.

He took two shells from the pocket of his barn coat, with the expertise of the champion skeet shooter he was, slid them into the barrels, and snapped the action into place with a sharp jerk that made a sickening click.

"Okay, you win," I said. "But tell me if I have it all figured out, first."

"Make it snappy. I don't want to miss my swim."

"Somehow you got Lawson to meet you at Makapuu Point. Blew his head off and dressed him in your clothes, counting on the similarities in your physique and your fraternity tattoos to make it seem it was you."

"What about the fingerprints," he asked, with a leer.

"That may have been the cleverest part of all. You bribed somebody to put Lawson's fingerprints onto a card with your name and then you had it put into your personnel file, so when Tommy Ford checked, they matched."

"I didn't have anyone do anything. Did it all myself," he said smugly. "I always told you that criminals tend to get caught because they have someone else do the dirty work. All that does is create a witness and another loose end."

"So, after you killed Lawson, you took the ferry to Kauai, where you had rented this house under an assumed name."

"It's under Heston and Ross. But I pay locally, so nothing ever gets sent to the office."

"Why not just skip out to the mainland right away?"

"You wouldn't make much of a criminal, Mac. I knew there would be way too much attention on who was leaving Oahu once my body was discovered. So, I had to go somewhere to lay low until things cooled off. I was due to catch a tramp steamer out of Lihue to Sydney the second week of December. Until the Japanese Navy screwed me over."

I said, "One morning Daniel Nakajima came strolling by your little cottage and laid eyes on you. He taught your daughter in school, so he recognized you immediately."

Hes nodded. "He saw me coming out of the pool. I ignored him and went inside, but I could tell he recognized me by the way he hurried on to the beach."

"The next day, you followed him to Lihue and bought a ticket on the same ferry, laying low somewhere below decks."

167

Hes nodded. "The cable tier."

"Good choice. Then you followed him off the boat and to his house. But how did you know where to lie in wait for him, that's the part I can't figure out."

"That's because you are underestimating my talents, old boy. You always did. I intercepted his letter. Once I knew he was on to me, I put him under constant surveillance. I can see most of the plantation from the telescope on my lanai. I waited until he left for Eleele, then just walked up and took the letter out of the mailbox, read it, and returned it to the box. I used the old knitting needle trick to get the letter out without breaking the seal. So, I knew where he was going and when he was going. I was on the ferry before he was and once we docked, I followed him home. I couldn't do it there, of course, But you can't get to the girlfriend's house without passing along that lane, unless you run down the middle of a busy highway."

Keep stalling. "So, you waited, and then you shot him, and got right back on the ferry and came back to Lihue."

"Good work, partner."

"But what about Tommy Ford? With the war on, you couldn't get back to Oahu to do your own dirty work on that one."

"That's where things started going downhill, which proves my theory about doing all the work yourself. I may as well tell you since you won't be going back. Bing Williams works for me. He took out Tommy when we realized he was getting too close to figuring it all out."

"Now it makes sense. I didn't think slitting throats was your style."

"It wouldn't have been my first choice, but that was just like Bing. It didn't leave any ballistic evidence, however, so it does have that to recommend it. What else can I do to satisfy your professional curiosity, Mac? It's getting late."

"You had Bing break into Marcia's house, because you realized there was an old fraternity photograph of you with Roger Lawson and that someone might connect the dots. Or, was it Money Branco?"

"Bing, naturally. It was too big a job for Money. You should consider doing this whole detective thing for a living, if you were not so soon to leave this mortal coil."

"What's your hurry? Let's finish the story, Bing hired Money Branco to lure me out Route 99 and lop my head off."

"Money Branco was perhaps not the best choice. More proof of my theory. Now I have a question for you."

"Okay."

"How did you figure out the dead body at Makapuu wasn't me?"

"Pineapple."

"What?"

"You didn't eat lunch with Roger Lawson, because we know you were down the coast meeting with Tommy Ford and promising him something big in the opium line for the following day." I used the "we" in hopes he would think I wasn't operating on my own, like the damned idiot I was.

"So?"

I swatted a mosquito and came away with a dot of blood on my hand. "So, you couldn't know that Lawson had eaten roast pork and pineapple for lunch, and that it would turn up in his stomach contents at the autopsy."

He was clearly impressed. "Well done, old boy. You must have remembered that I hate the stuff. Well done, indeed. I would reproach myself for the slipup, but as you rightly point out, I had no way of knowing. And I needed the face-to-face with Ford so he would think—so everyone would think—I had been bumped off for nosing into the opium trade. In the end, none of it matters, so I'm not sure I'm willing to concede it was a slip up. De minimus non curat lex, old man."

"We're talking about lives, not trifles."

"Always the *haole* do-gooder, aren't you, Mac?"

I let it go. After all, I had nothing to lose but my life.

"Oh, one more thing. What was in the safe at Marcia's?"

"A red herring." He laughed, softly at first, then louder and louder, until it dissolved in a fit of coughing. He wiped his eyes, "Sometimes, I kill myself, Mac. Get it?" He laughed again, but I could tell his heart wasn't really in it.

From somewhere close by, I heard the call of a pueo, the protector: a rapid Who-Who-Who-Who-WHO. It may have been my imagination, but it sounded almost like a signal. The sound of the mosquitoes fell suddenly in pitch to a deeper, bass note, then rose in intensity, until it reminded me of the night I had spent not so far from where we stood. Hundreds of dragonflies had come out at dusk to feed on the insects attracted by our bonfire. Their collective wings had made a vast hum, like an electric transformer.

Abruptly, the hum grew louder still. Hes turned toward it, just as the sound resolved itself into a high-performance motorcycle. It grew rapidly closer. A look of recognition mixed with utter dread came over Hes' face. I heard the sound of a gunshot and saw a red wound appear on Hes' arm. He cried out and dropped the shotgun, clutching at his arm.

The bike was right on top of us now. I could feel the vibrations of its powerful engine through the earth. I heard the brakes give a whine that mingled with Hes' cries of pain. He opened his mouth to say something.

At the edge of my vision, I saw the shape of a human figure and then the merest whisper of a sound the Japanese call *Tachikaze*—sword wind—ending with a muffled thump, as Hes' head was cleanly severed from the rest of him.

His body seemed to fall in slow motion, first to his knees, then completely from sight. After a pause in which I couldn't draw breath, I heard a lightly accented voice say, with formal politeness, "Honor is restored, Ross-san. Someone will come to collect you, sir. Stay put if you please."

#

CHAPTER 12

I gave the Kauai County Sheriff and his stenographer the whole story, while we were still at the scene. Well, not the whole story. I left out the voice saying honor had been restored. And, when the sheriff asked who killed Hes, I said it must surely be the man they called The Chairman. After all, the reason Hes came to Kauai was to hide out from him, until he could slip away to Australia. The stenographer hurried ahead of us to Lihue to turn it into a statement.

On the ride back I was treated to a police escort. I guess, since I was the only one who could make their case, they were a little nervous until I signed on the dotted line.

Turns out, having an escort isn't much fun. The pace is far too sedate, and its considered unseemly to pass the lead car. When we made it to headquarters, I called Rogers. His assistant said Jack was on the horn with President Roosevelt.

"Well, in that case, don't interrupt him," I said, but the assistant didn't care for the joke, so I gave him the low down and suggested, ever so gently, they should be the ones to put the cuffs on Bing. I was sorry I wouldn't be there to see it.

Next, I cabled Marcia, "Avoid radio and newspapers until I get there this evening. All is well." And to Koga, "Hes Heston, found to be living on Kauai, has died at the hands of an unknown assailant. Before his death, he confessed to the murders of Nakajima, Lawson, and to directing the homicide of Det. Ford, at the hands of Bing Williams. The murders were committed in furtherance of Heston's scheme to start a new life in Australia."

I called Miss K. She had two messages and read them to me in her formal way.

"The first message is from Mrs. Marcia Heston and reads as follows, 'I believe Major Lawson was in the missing photograph, along with Hes and two of their fraternity brothers. Please call when you get back.' End of message, Mr. Ross.'"

"Thank you."

"And the second is from our dear Oz. It reads, 'Tommy Espinoza, alias Tommy Two-Toes, located and delivered to Mr. Sears' office, where he signed a statement.' End of message.'"

"Thanks, dear. Take the rest of the day off."

"Oh, boss!"

I put down the phone and realized the Sheriff had been waiting deferentially, with my statement in hand. Being treated so nicely by local authorities was going to take some getting used to.

It took a while for me to make it out of the sheriff's office. It seemed like everyone wanted to shake my hand, which was odd because I hadn't brought Hes to justice. Left to my own devices, I'd still be sitting in the bottom of a tiger pit with a sore ankle and no prospects.

I drove up a block and over a couple, just to get some space from it all, then pulled into the first diner I saw. Suddenly, I was ravenously hungry. While I ate my "Aloha Burger," with pineapple, of course, I thought about what Daniel's uncle would say if he knew I had found the ghost.

#

For five solid hours, I did nothing but stare blankly at the sea flowing past the hull of the *Charon*. Kauai receded, leaving us in the open ocean. Before the seas began to kick up, we were visited by a pod of *kohola* whales. When they surfaced, they exhaled their steamy breath with a loud sigh that felt like it should be mine.

Namakaokahai, goddess of the sea, had begun to whip up her winter swells, but the motion of the ship felt like an old friend I hadn't seen in a while. It got dark before we reached Oahu, but I could feel the city looming out there in the blackout.

Right on schedule, the dock lights of Pearl hove into view.

Nalani was waiting at the end of the gangplank, standing near a troop of photographers and a couple of reporters, most of whom I knew. I pushed the bike down the ramp. When I got near the end, the photographers readied their big Speed Graphic cameras.

"Look right here, Mac."

I smiled instinctively, thinking, *What a chump I am.* The flash bulb popped and sizzled with a frying sound.

"Hey, can you get on the bike?"

I said, "No I can't. Sorry guys. And I won't have anything to say until I've spoken with the proper authorities." I had played these games before. The reporters went away with an air of disappointment. I put the bike on its stand and held Nalani close. She smelled like heaven above.

The boat emptied, leaving us alone amid the cries of the stevedores, "Hold it there," "Bring it down," "Take it away." When we finally pulled ourselves apart, Nalani said, "Let's go home. I'll cook for *you* tonight."

"That sounds wonderful, but first I have to go tell Marcia her husband has been killed. Again."

"Would it help if I go with you?"

"Oh, God, yes. Would you?"

#

Despite my reticence, the story was on the front pages the next day, and it was far too bloody to be anywhere but above the fold. *The Star-Bulletin* went first, with "Death Follows Honolulu PI Mac Ross, But Only for the Bad Guys." Not bad.

The Advertiser countered, as usual, with a more somber telling: "Private Detective Uncovers Partner's Murder." The story didn't lack any of the bloody details but focused on the ironic fact that Hes was his own murderer the first time around. A helpful sidebar reminded readers of others from the Territory who had faked their own deaths, as if it was a trend we needed to guard against.

Luckily for me, I had to come back down to earth quickly. By that afternoon, I was in a conference room at the University of Hawaii, freshly shaven and in my best suit and tie, a businesslike fedora lying on the seat beside me. Across the table was an academic type who had no idea I was in all the papers and who, if he had known, would have doubtless found it all a bit distasteful.

"Thank you for coming, Mr. Ross."

"My pleasure."

He looked at the file in front of him. "You're here to speak on behalf of Osvaldo Ferrer, is that correct?"

"Yes, sir, I am."

"So, tell me, Mr. Ross, why, as the Dean of the Department of Criminology, I should grant young Mr. Ferrer late admission to our program. We already have a full complement for next fall."

"Because he's too smart for the Police Academy, that's why. He has an instinct for the work. He's bright and eager, and he has a strong ethical sense."

"I see," he said, with the barest scintilla of appreciation.

"He's done some work for me, in fact—"

"In your private investigations?"

"Yes, sir."

His peevish face grew even less inviting. "And you believe that qualifies him for our award-winning criminology program?"

"No, sir. Not by itself. But it gave him the opportunity to demonstrate his considerable potential. If you admit him, Doctor, you won't be sorry."

"Technically, Mr. Ross, I'm to be address as 'Dean,' but in any event, if I had a nickel for everyone—"

"Look, I'm sure that's the case, but this time, the candidate is the real McCoy."

He closed the file, "Very well, Mr. Ross. I'll make a note of your endorsement and I am sure our admissions committee will give it all due weight."

"Thank you, Dean. I should just mention that he has had overtures from other institutions. The University of California seems the most enthusiastic. I understand they have a serious program of their own."

His sour face never changed. He extended his hand in a limp handshake. "Yes, indeed they do."

#

I kept the suit on for dinner with Koga that evening. Nalani and I purposefully flaunted the curfew, relying on the special juju of my night driving pass, with silent gratitude to Tommy Ford. The butler showed us in. We changed into our list slippers and Koga rose to greet us, kissing Nalani on both cheeks, in a decidedly un-Japanese manner.

All through the exquisite dinner—filets emincé, buttered balsamic mushrooms, roasted green beans with Japanese chilis —Koga avoided talking about the case. When the cloth was drawn, he served us each a snifter of brandy and passed around his Partagas. To my surprise, Nalani took one and expertly lit it.

She caught me staring. "What?" My grandmother loves them. She taught me."

Throughout the evening, Koga studiously skirted any conversational path that might reveal exactly how much he knew about Hes' death or last days on Kauai. I played right along, puffing contentedly on my Cuban cigar and putting off smoke like Steamboat Willie.

Koga said, "Thank you for the courtesy of your cable. I am grateful to you for keeping us informed. Mr. Sato is very pleased with the outcome."

"Well, I'm not really entitled to collect the bonus—no arrest and conviction, I'm afraid."

"No, no. We are in your debt, I do assure you, sir. This seems like the perfect moment for us to repay it." He took an envelope from the breast pocket of his suit coat and handed it to me with a flourish.

"Your fee and agreed upon bonus, with a bit extra as

an acknowledgement, inadequate though it may be, of your extraordinary performance in this matter. I am also pleased to say you can expect a case of Rittenhouse Rye Whiskey. I believe that's your favorite. Oh, and one of the champagne. They'll be delivered, of course. I thought it might be a bit awkward for you to take them home on the motorbike."

#

The champagne didn't last a day, because the next afternoon, we threw a party in the big upstairs room at Wo Fat. Everyone was there and everyone was mightily thirsty. Koga, Ochoa, Oz, Arando, Pederson, and Grimes. Mary Nell and Kai. Even Dave Summers dropped by.

About halfway into the festivities, Marcia Heston came strolling in, smiling, and looking at peace with the world again, which did my heart good. Nalani joined from work, with her mother in tow. She was a radiant, lovely woman, with an air of incipient mischief and the same intelligent eyes I had fallen in love with.

"I told Nalani, last year, that she would find someone. But in my dreams, he rode a roan horse."

I took her by the arm and led her to the window, pointing down to the Indian, my Rocinante, where the valet was watching it. "I do. And there it is." She was puzzled, but only for an instant before insisting that she had been right all along.

Vassar and Warren Sears walked through the door. She was wearing a good deal of makeup, which was not her style, but smiling broadly. We hugged.

In answer to my question, she said, "All charges dropped, Mac. I drive my enemies before me through the streets in chains. Well, he does," pointing to Sears who smiled coyly, obviously taken with his client.

I laughed. "Even the profanity charge?"

Warren piped in, "Even that. Of course, it didn't hurt that the prosecution's chief witness had just been taken into federal custody, thanks to you, Mac. Although I'd like to think we had 'em beaten regardless."

"So," Vassar said, "As soon as the judge banged his gavel, me and this little tiger man here marched our asses over to the county clerk's office and filed a civil suit for damages in the amount of $100,000."

"We don't expect to be awarded that much, mind you," Sears said, ever the lawyer.

Gus came into the room, playing "Sweat Joy" on his accordion. When it wound down, I got everyone's attention.

"Thank you all for coming. It may seem strange that we celebrate, when some are not here to celebrate with us. Good men, like Roger Lawson and my old partner Tommy Ford. But we do celebrate because those who robbed them of life have been brought to account."

"Hear, hear," Grimes said, carried away with the emotion of the moment and the good champagne.

"So, here's to my protectors," I said with a gesture to my comrades. "And to my clients, Koga-san and Sato-san, for their very active help and support. Kanpai!"

Koga bowed and dutifully drank up.

"Here's to all my friends. Every last one of you. Cheers."

They drank to themselves with enthusiasm.

"Finally," I said, "here's to my love." This drew a collective, "Ah," from the room. "Thank you for going on this adventure with me, and for giving our love a chance. Here's to many more adventures," I said, kissing her, to wild applause.

THE END

Made in the USA
Las Vegas, NV
05 October 2024

96321149R10098